KT-103-778

BIRCH COMMON

Barbara Cooper has recently been widowed at the shockingly early age of 42. She lives in the idyllic village of Texbury on a green known as Birch Common, but life for Barbara is grey and meaningless at present. Things look up when, visiting London, she has a chance encounter with Bryan Payne who kindly rescues her after a fall in the street. He's a travel courier and specialises in escorting guided tours of India. This lights a spark in Barbara's imagination. Can she trust him? Dare she love again?

BIRCH COMMON

BIRCH COMMON

by

Rose Boucheron

WARWICKSHIRE
COUNTY LIBRARY

CONTROL No.

Magna Large Print Books
Long Preston, North Yorkshire,
BD23 4ND, England.

British Library Cataloguing in Publication Data.

Boucheron, Rose
    Birch Common.

    A catalogue record of this book is
    available from the British Library

    ISBN   0-7505-2028-0

First published in Great Britain in 2002
by Judy Piatkus (Publishers) Ltd.

Copyright © 2002 by Rose Boucheron

Cover illustration © John Hancock by arrangement with
P.W.A. International Ltd.

The moral right of the author has been asserted

Published in Large Print 2003 by arrangement with
Piatkus Books Ltd.

All Rights reserved. No part of this publication may be
reproduced, stored in a retrieval system, or transmitted in any
form or by any means, electronic, mechanical, photocopying,
recording or otherwise without the prior permission of the
Copyright owner.

Magna Large Print is an imprint of Library Magna Books Ltd.

Printed and bound in Great Britain by
T.J. (International) Ltd., Cornwall, PL28 8RW

All the characters in this book are
fictitious and any resemblance
to real persons, living or dead,
is entirely coincidental.

Chapter One

The picturesque village of Texbury centred around a common, known to the locals as Birch Common. In reality it was a large open space surrounded by houses of various ages in an odd but attractive assortment of architectural styles. These included a row of Victorian cottages, several Edwardian villas, four extremely well-built brick houses, reputedly Lutyens, Kirby Lodge, a grand Victorian house with its own arboretum, and a Georgian house set well back off the road behind a gracious carriage drive.

A pretty hotel stood at the edge of the common. It was much used for commercial conferences and also for illicit weekends, principally because it was not too far from London, and on the edge of 'the country'.

A road ran around the common, wide enough for sightseers' buses and coaches and the residents' ubiquitous Land Rovers, one lane leading back to London and the other to the west.

Village lore had it that just prior to World

War One, a disastrous fire had overtaken the common which at that time was almost completely covered in heather and gorse. The fire burned for fourteen days and nights, and afterwards the blackened earth sprouted tiny seedlings of birch which had not been seen there before, oak and elm being indigenous to that part of the country. It gave the piece of ground a glade-like appearance and afterwards it became known as Birch Common.

Barbara Cooper, who lived in a small detached Edwardian villa called Heather-side, knew few people in the houses surrounding her, having moved there four years previously when her husband's parents had died. Before that, she and William had lived in a flat in Texbury, and since she'd had a job in the local bookshop she had not really become part of the social scene on Birch Common. Before her marriage she had been a librarian in the public library at Woodside, but when they'd moved to Texbury she'd taken the job in the bookshop to be nearer home.

William's parents had bought the villa upon marrying and had lived in it for the rest of their lives. William had been an only child and he and Barbara knew they were extremely fortunate to have inherited the house with its well-cared for little garden and its prime position on the edge of the common. Now, with William's recent death, and her being made redundant just two weeks ago, the bookshop having closed down, Barbara knew she must look for something else to do. Not that there was exactly a social whirl on Birch Common, for they were a disparate group of people who kept very much to themselves apart from Constance Pargetter-Wilson, the local do-gooder, whom you could be sure to find on your doorstep at any hour of the day or night collecting for charity. Most of the neighbours knew, of course, that William Cooper had died, some of them remembered him as a small boy and duly made their condolences, but there it stayed.

On this Monday evening, having just returned from a weekend with friends in London, Barbara opened the casement doors to let in the fresh air from the garden, seeing the roses so carefully nurtured by William's father now left to fend for themselves unless Tom the general handyman in the area could give her an hour. He also cut the tiny lawn when necessary. She had taken over where William had left off, but gardening didn't come as naturally to her as it had to her husband. She quite liked it but recognised the need to get herself settled into some sort of job before she could really enjoy more relaxing pursuits. She heard dogs barking on the common and knew that might be the answer, to get herself one, but before that she must make up her mind about her future.

Upstairs she ran the bath and sprinkled in scented salts, her mind still on the weekend she had spent with her old school friend Rosemary and family. She threw her torn tights into the waste bin, and eyed the graze on her knee caused by the fall she'd suffered. Not too bad – it could have been worse. She thought again about the man who had helped her. Not only had he rescued her like a Good Samaritan, he'd been kindness itself, even buying her tea – oh, it had been lovely to have a helpful man around, she thought wistfully. Good-looking, too.

As she lay in the bath, she reflected back on her day and the startling change in her feelings it had brought about.

At breakfast time, when she was about to leave London, the sun had shone palely through the long narrow window of the house in Connaught Street, lighting up the table with its empty dishes, rack containing a lone slice of toast, pilfered fruit bowl.

Rosemary studied Barbara with eyes full of concern as she picked up her handbag and, with one arm round her hostess's shoulders, leaned forward to kiss her and thank her for the two-night stay.

'Are you sure you want to leave so early? It's only ten-thirty.' Rosemary's green eyes were kind. 'You're not going to Marylebone already – not going straight home surely?'

Barbara tried to look calm and decisive. Could Rosemary see the doubt in her eyes? Why would she go home? What would she do there, for goodness' sake?

'No, I'm going to Kensington,' she said on the spur of the moment, thinking, was she? Well, why not? It was years since she had been to Kensington. She had stayed here for the weekend with Rosemary, her best friend from schooldays, and her husband Don. Now they had to get on with their lives – as she had.

'Then I can give you a lift to Notting Hill Gate. Cassie has a ballet class there at eleven-fifteen.'

'Thank you, Roz. That's nice.

Rosemary and Don were absorbed in their

own lives and those of their children, Cassie and Hugh, and why would they not be? Don avoided looking at Barbara. Kind as he was, she knew what he was thinking. You have to go it alone, Babs – he was the only one who called her that – we've done all we can and we're there for you if you need us but...

She knew she looked awful, her face drawn after losing so much weight; the slender legs which had always been her best feature even thinner now. She tended to slump nowadays instead of walking tall.

'Got everything, Barbara?' She picked up her holdall containing nightie, toothbrush, overnight things. A pathetic little assortment it seemed to her.

Don kissed her and Hugh hugged her, they were such darlings, waving to her from the door as she and Cassie joined Rosemary in the car which made for Hyde Park and was soon in the thick of the Bayswater Road, getting caught up in traffic on this Monday morning. Don worked from home. How she envied Rosemary.

'There are some sales – you could look round,' her friend said. 'Buy something nice – something special – treat yourself.'

'Yes, good idea. I will,' Barbara said, feeling sick inside and hoping Roz could not see

14

that she was visibly shaking.

When they came to the top of Church Street the car drew to a halt. 'I can only stop a moment, I'm on a double yellow,' Rosemary said, leaning across to kiss her. 'You could walk or get a bus from here.'

''Bye, Auntie Barbara,' Cassie called from the back seat and blew her a kiss.

'Thank you, I'm fine, I'll walk.' And getting out of the car, almost falling she felt so weak, closing the door with a bang, she watched them drive away. She had never felt so alone. What would people do if she collapsed here? Leave her on the pavement, as she had read they did in New York? Send for an ambulance? But that was silly, of course. She was not going to collapse on the pavement, however much she wished she could.

She stopped outside an estate agent's window and looked at the photographs. Heavens! Seven hundred thousand ... a million ... two point five million. Where was it her mother used to live? She had had a little flat during the forties when she'd worked at the War Office. It was a basement flat in Church Street somewhere. She had shown Barbara once, but now she couldn't recall the name of the apartment block.

15

She felt she wanted to die. To die, just like that. Of course, she'd never do anything about it, not actually kill herself. For one thing, she hadn't the courage. But really the law was wrong. If you'd had enough of life, why not? What harm did it do anyone else? It wasn't as if they'd had children – she and William. Why make it such a stigma to put an end to an empty existence?

It was almost a year since he had died. Shouldn't she be over it by now? There were times she'd almost thought she was, but she always came back to this mood of hopelessness, this loneliness. Walking past the antique shops, she remembered coming here in better times when she was young and happy with so many things to do: her job, her husband, her life. Her days had been full then. What good was she to anyone now?

She had never imagined her future being like this, widowed at forty-two. And who would have thought she would have gone to pieces, become so lost, so bereft? Where was all her old strength – her courage?

As people passed her she saw that a lot of them were alone, just like her. She forgot just how many but several millions of people lived alone, she had read, and from choice many of them.

She had reached the crossing at the bottom of Church Street and saw Kensington High Street ahead. What had happened to Derry and Toms and its roof garden? How long was it since she had been here? And so many people, a crowd it seemed like, waiting to cross the road. She might be knocked down by a bus and then people would crowd eagerly around. 'I don't think she saw it,' they would say. And she would lie there, lifeless, in her pale green suit.

But somehow she was crossing safely with the others. There was a family ahead. I could tag on to them, she thought, be with them, enter into conversation with them. Don't you see, I'm lonely for someone to talk to?

They all seemed to be madly rushing to the shops for as she could see some clearances were in full swing. People were buying blankets, television sets, mobile phones. It still went on, then. But she needed nothing. She had a perfectly good home, fully equipped, there was absolutely nothing she needed. Apart from someone to talk to.

Going into Barker's, she thought, I'll have a coffee, and saw the entrance to a cafe downstairs. She was halfway down when the thought came to her, I need something stronger than coffee, I need a drink, something to pull me round. Arriving at the bottom, she went straight over to the up escalator. Not a pub, she decided, not as an unaccompanied woman. She came to a wine bar. Outside a sign read: SAND-WICHES SERVED HERE. That would do. It wasn't much of a place but at least it was warm inside and she could have a reviving drink.

Sitting herself down, she picked up a menu. A girl wandered over, all of sixteen and pretty, with a short skirt and thick black tights, her hair frizzed out around her head. She smiled at her solitary customer. I bet she thinks I'm ninety, Barbara thought.

'A glass of red wine, please,' she said, scanning the menu. Nothing really appealed and yet she had had no breakfast to speak of, and knew she should eat.

Sausage sandwich, she read. What was a sausage sandwich? Novel, at any rate. William had loved sausages, but she hadn't bought them as often as she should. Her mother had never approved of sausages, and Barbara had grown up feeling wary of them.

'A sausage sandwich,' she said, 'please.' For she was of the generation that is automatically polite.

The trouble was, she reflected, William had done everything for her: paid the bills, looked after the household accounts, mended everything that went wrong, serviced the car and seen to the income tax. What was she but a hanger on? Now there were terrifying mounds of post which kept coming – gas bills, electricity bills, insurance – and she had always been a dunderhead about money. She had to search through files to find out how much they had paid before. Were they overcharging her now – did she care? And the toaster had finally given up the ghost, and there was no saying, 'William, the fuse has gone – can you see to it?' Not any more.

With his going like that – in five minutes, from a massive heart attack – she hadn't been prepared. There wasn't even time to say goodbye.

That terrible call from his office to the bookshop, and then the journey to St Thomas's Hospital where they had taken him – but she had arrived too late, he was already dead. Could she possibly have imagined when they'd parted that morning it would be the last time she would see him alive?

Just forty-seven and never been ill.

'Toasted or untoasted? Brown or white bread?' the girl asked, coming back, and brought her down to earth by placing the glass of wine in front of her.

'Brown untoasted, please,' said Barbara, and took a sip of the red wine which proved to be quite good.

I don't suppose anyone realises I'm going mad, she thought. I'm probably having a nervous breakdown. Bonkers, that's the word they use today. I'm just no good on my own. If I were of this generation I'd take it all in my stride, but I'm not. And William and I had the perfect marriage – or did we? I wasn't stupid before I married him, was I? How she hated it now when the cistern leaked and the plumber didn't arrive, or the gas bill looked to be twice as much as it should be. She had always loathed figures anyway. Do I need an accountant? she wondered. A handyman? No, she thought. I just need William.

She had turned the water off in the empty house where she still expected to find him waiting for her when she got home. She had seen that the electricity was off too. How did other women manage? Very efficiently – she had seen them. She had obviously been hopelessly spoiled and now it was time to pull herself together and assert her independence. Think of all the poor people worse off than her, in pain with terminal illnesses. She did, all the time, though it made no difference.

She was past her sell-by-date, that was the trouble. Forty-two might as well have been sixty-two for all the options open to her. How she would have loved children! But William had never wanted them and anyway she never seemed to get pregnant, even when she tried.

Shouldn't she have got over that by now?

She drank some more wine, and the waitress brought the sandwich. When Barbara opened it gingerly with her knife three midget sausages lay there side by side like baby mice. She wanted to laugh, it was so incongruous. Three little baby mice. Of course, she couldn't eat them. She finished her red wine, feeling a sudden surge of renewed strength and confidence.

You're not going bonkers, she told herself. You were strong when it happened. You didn't collapse or faint. Think about it. You've been married for twenty years to a man who did everything for you. And now you don't like being alone. Of course you don't, no one would, but you're definitely not going mad.

She stood up and paid the bill, walked outside only to find it was pouring – and she had no umbrella.

She walked along until she came back to Barker's where there were dozens of umbrellas, short ones, stumpy ones, long elegant designs, and decided on a telescopic one which would always be useful. Then, hurrying on her way, she walked through blinding rain to Kensington High Street station and made her way to the Underground.

As the train rumbled along she smiled at the memory of those sausages, then thought back to her weekend with Rosemary and Don. What a nice family they were – she was lucky to have them to go to for the occasional town weekend. Still, she mustn't overdo it, grow to rely on them, she must find something else to do – a hobby. But she was going to be a long time getting round to it, she knew.

She had come up the escalator and was making her way from Baker Street to Marylebone. The rain had stopped but the roads were wet and slippery. Crossing Dorset Street, she tripped and fell head-long. Only the quick thinking of a man coming towards her managed to save her from the traffic. He helped to steady her and brush her down. She looked down at her torn tights, at the graze on her knee, and then up to find a tall man of about fifty looking at her sympathetically. 'Are you all right? Stand still for a moment, it's always a shock when you fall.'

He had his hand at her elbow, supporting her, for which she was grateful. She felt absurdly shaken, and leaned against the railings weakly. He produced a large white handkerchief to stem the slight bleeding on her knee and could tell by her dazed expression that she had suffered a shock. She was as pale as a lily, too.

'Were you making for the station?' he asked kindly.

She nodded. 'Yes, Marylebone.'

'I've just come from there but let me walk you back?'

'No, no. It's all right, thank you,' she said, feeling embarrassed.

'No trouble — it's only a step.' His manner was so calm and unruffled. He had a kindly face and spoke as if he was used to looking after people. Perhaps he was a doctor, she thought, though somehow he didn't look like one.

Arriving at the station, he steered her into the small cafe.

'A nice cup of tea will pull you round,' he said, leaving her sitting at an empty table and returning in no time with two cups of steaming hot tea.

'Nothing like a cup of tea,' he said as she began to apologise again. 'Sugar?'

'No, thanks,' said Barbara, the first sip of tea reviving her. How foolish she felt – all this fuss because she couldn't look where she was going. She looked down at her knee. 'It's nothing,' she said with a thin smile. 'Thank you very much, you've been so kind.'

'Not at all,' he said. 'I suppose I'm used to helping travellers. I'm a courier by profession and used to lending a helping hand.'

She looked into smiling eyes of a deep dark brown, with little laughter lines at their corners.

'How interesting,' she said, finding that she meant it. Everything about this calm, competent, good-humoured man was undeniably appealing.

'It is,' he said. 'I love it. I never tire of it – and I've been doing it for some years now.'

It sounded very romantic to Barbara.

'Where do you go?'

'India, mainly,' he said. 'I'm off again to-morrow as it happens.'

And at once she conjured up visions of India as she saw it: brilliant sun, jewel colours, lakes, palaces and deserts.

'How wonderful,' she sighed.

'Yes, it is. It's a fascinating country – have you ever been?'

She shook her head. 'No, never, but I'd love to go.'

'Then make up your mind to do it,' he said. 'And no time like the present.' Her mind began to race. He finished his tea and pushed back his chair. 'Well, if you're sure you'll be all right...'

'Yes, thank you so much for your help – I don't even know your name. And thank you for the tea.'

'Bryan Payne,' he said, holding out his hand.

'Barbara Cooper,' she said, and watched him walk out of the station.

Afterwards, in the Ladies Room, she sponged her knee and tidied herself. What a sight she looked – pale and strained and grubby. You're a mess, she told herself. So much for a reviving weekend away.

Her train pulled out of the station and soon they were coming to the edge of the countryside. It was the height of spring, with green coming into fields and hedgerows, the trees in full leaf, the lake at Denham with tiny boats on it – a lovely time of year. She might just take her supper into the garden this evening...

She thought about her rescuer, Bryan. How kind he'd been, and how interesting to work in India. All her life she'd wanted to go there. Almost every year she had asked William if they could go to India, her lifelong dream, and every year he'd said, 'Yes, why not?'

But they never had. That last year, it was strange, he'd said, 'Truth to tell, Barbara, I've never wanted to go to India.'

'Then why didn't you say?' she'd asked him. 'Oh, you should have said.' As if it would have made any difference.

'I didn't want to disappoint you.' So they had gone to France instead – again.

Now here she was, widowed and unemployed, beginning to revive that dream, seriously contemplating the voyage of a lifetime.

Well, what was wrong with dreaming?

And what was the worst that could happen to her? She might fall ill, be raped, even murdered, she supposed. But so what?

Almost anything was better than the empty life she was living now.

At the bookshop where she had worked they'd have said she was mad. Or would they? Maybe instead they'd have told her, 'Get a life – it's time you did something different.'

There she was again, brooding about madness – but this was a different kind of madness, wasn't it? An urge to indulge herself just once in her life, to grant herself one joyful thing in a patch of desolation.

Out of the bath, she dried herself and put some Savlon on the graze on her knee. What a fuss about nothing it had been. And that kind man Bryan was off to India tomorrow. How she envied him.

Still, there was nothing to stop her going, was there? Why was she always so scared of life? She was a free agent – more's the pity. She had liked being married, having a husband, but now she could please herself. She suddenly found herself wondering what Bryan's wife was like. Not much fun for her if her husband spent half his time in India.

Still, better than not having one at all.

She put on trousers and a cool cotton shirt. She would take a stroll on the common, and then before dinner she might just open a good bottle of wine. She smiled as she remembered those little mice in the sausage sandwich.

Get a grip, Barbara, she told herself with renewed resolution. Stop frittering your life away on the small daily things and really *do* something for once.

Chapter Two

On this balmy evening, still with her head full of thoughts of India, Barbara took a stroll out on to the common which she sometimes did if it was quiet. The air was fresh and she breathed in deeply, appreciating the country scents of the grass and trees as she walked across to the other side with its little coppice of silver birches then returned along the path worn into the grass by frequent use. Her route took her past the Lutyens houses, one of which belonged to Constance Pargetter-Wilson. She stopped to admire the fabulous garden then walked on by the semi-detached Edwardian villas near her own.

There were new people in one of them, a couple with a small boy. She had seen them walking on the common on a Sunday, sometimes accompanied by an older woman, perhaps the boy's grandmother.

In the front garden, which still had its old wrought-iron railings and decorative gate, closed now, she saw a boy lying on the ground playing with a toy train. Hearing her approach, he looked up and down again, then getting to his feet he ran the little train along the wall, at which it promptly fell off and Barbara retrieved it for him.

'Thank you.' Looking up at her were two bright blue eyes set in a serious little face. He must be about seven years old.

'I know you,' he said. 'You live along there in Heatherside, don't you?'

She was surprised that he knew this.

'Yes, that's right.'

'I know all the names of the houses on the common.'

'What – every one?' She sounded surprised.

'Yes,' he said. 'We live at Sunnyside – look, you can see it painted on the fanlight. My dad told me the name of that little window over the door. 'Course, the paint's a bit worn out now.'

'But you can still read it,' Barbara confirmed as a young woman came out of the house to see who her son was talking to.

'Oh, hello – Mrs Cooper, isn't it?' She smiled at Barbara. She was extremely pretty with short fair hair and blue eyes just like her son's.

Barbara liked her on sight. 'Barbara

Cooper,' she said, and held out her hand.

'I'm Vivien McKay – Viv,' she added, taking Barbara's hand. 'And this is Ben, my son. Say hello to Mrs Cooper, Ben.'

'Hello.' And he went straight back to his train.

'We haven't been here long – just a year,' Viv said. 'My husband was transferred here. We're from Cheshire originally.'

'Oh, that's nice,' Barbara said. 'I know Cheshire, I have an aunt living there.'

'Yes, it's very different from here.'

'And have you settled in?'

'Yes, I suppose so. It seems awfully small after our other house, but property is so expensive down south.'

'I know. I was lucky enough to inherit the house from my in-laws – or at least my husband did. Then, when he died, it came to me.'

'Oh, I know, someone told me. Gosh, he must have been quite young.'

'Yes, forty-seven.'

'You must get awfully lonely,' Viv sympathised, 'but I expect you work, don't you? I have a job in London – my mother looks after Ben for me. Fortunately she's not too far away, one of the reasons we came here, so that's a bonus. What about you?'

'Well, I did, but the bookshop where I worked had to close two weeks ago so now I'm looking for something else to do. Still, things could be worse.'

'You must come and have coffee with me,' Viv said, taking her son's hand. 'I'll give you a call. Come on, Ben, time you came in and had your bath.'

''Bye,' he called out as he made his way reluctantly inside. What a day, thought Barbara. First the man at the station, and now Viv. She seemed really nice. No doubt about it, things were looking up. And to think that only this morning she'd moment-arily contemplated throwing herself under a bus in High Street Ken.

After his bath, Ben was allowed to stay up for a while to see his father before going to bed.

On this particular evening Dad was in an extremely good mood. There was an air of suppressed excitement about him, but only Ben's mother noticed that. Ben himself was deeply engrossed in his Lego and busy building a special kind of tractor. His father had picked him up and held him high over his head, and Ben had had the distinct feeling that if he hadn't been there Dad would have picked Mum up too and whirled her round.

Busy as he was he could hear them – or rather his father – talking animatedly. Dad was waving his arms about and Ben guessed it must be about something important. There was a lot of talk about money, and his mother said, 'Shh!' several times, but then she didn't speak at all and his father went on and on. Ben looked up to find his mother staring at the wall, looking upset.

His father sounded uneasy. 'Viv – aren't you going to congratulate me?' he asked. 'Tell me how clever I am?'

Ben looked away, staring hard at the wheels of his tractor.

'Shh, George,' his mother said. 'We'll talk about it when I come down. Say goodnight to Daddy, Ben, it's bedtime.'

He was quite glad to get to bed although he would have liked to know what they were talking about. He didn't want them to argue – he hated it when they did.

'Goodnight, Daddy,' he said. 'Can I leave the layout there until the morning?'

'Of course you can,' his father said, noticing the fine yellow tractor that Ben was clutching to him.

'Are you taking that up with you?'

'Yes.'

'That's great, Ben,' his father said. 'I'd no idea you were getting so good.'

Ben's eyes shone as his father leaned down to kiss him.

'Goodnight, Sunny Jim.' Dad often called him that.

His mother seemed to spend a long time tucking him in and reading him a story as if she didn't want to go back downstairs, but eventually she turned out the light and closed the door behind her.

Downstairs, George McKay had poured out a glass of wine for each of them.

'Good health,' he said. He had simmered down a little, but the gleam of excitement was still in his eyes as he waited for Viv to say something.

She took her time about settling herself in an armchair facing him. Then she looked him in the eye.

'George, I'm sure it's a feather in your cap, and it sounds wonderful, but Ben and I couldn't possibly go and live in America.'

'Why ever not?'

'Well – because,' Viv said uneasily. 'It may not matter to you, George, but I want my son to be educated in England. And besides I like my job here, and my home.'

34

He snorted. 'But we're a family, for heaven's sake! You knew I was applying for the position.'

'To be honest, I really didn't think you stood a chance of getting it.'

'Oh, thanks!'

Upstairs Ben could hear the low murmuring. They didn't often argue so this made it doubly unsettling. Still, everything would be all right in the morning, he thought, clutching his Teddy tightly.

Returning to Heatherside, Barbara felt unusually pleased with her day. She had been out of a job for two weeks, and knew for the first time the pleasures of not having to get up early each morning. She had thought after her weekend with Rosemary and Don that she would start to look around for something else in earnest, but somehow the events of today had changed all that. After meeting Viv and that nice little boy, she supposed if she had time to herself she might build up more of a social life. She didn't really have one as yet, never had. William had not been a mixer – he'd had no hobbies except gardening and had worked hard at his insurance job in the City. Once they were home in the evening their time was taken up with cooking meals, catching up with the papers, talking to each other about the events of their day. At weekends they would go walking in the surrounding countryside. Very occasionally they went to a show in town or the local cinema. She supposed on reflection that her life had always been dull by comparison with some people's. The owner of the bookshop, a retired lady teacher, had belonged to a dozen different societies: the operatic society, drama society, the art appreciation class, the National Trust. There was no end to her activities and she was a woman of sixty-four.

Barbara sighed. Yes, she had let herself get into a rut, and looked set to continue doing so unless she really took herself in hand.

Aware that some new avenues must be explored, she let herself into the house and closed the door behind her, immediately bolting and locking it just as William and his family had always done over the years.

It was still light on his late-spring evening, and she had barely closed the door when the bell rang. Startled, she jumped, wondering who it could be – she had so few callers.

Through the frosted glass she could see it was a woman. Barbara unlocked and unbolted the door and peered round it.

The rather large well-dressed lady standing on the doorstep looked familiar. She smiled warmly at Barbara who could see that she held a sheaf of programmes to her very feminine bosom.

'Good evening, Mrs Cooper.'

'Good evening, Mrs Pargetter-Wilson.'

It was she who lived in the Lutyens house whose garden Barbara had stood and admired this very evening.

'How do you do? Won't you come in?' Barbara invited her.

'No, my dear, I'm on my way round the common hoping to entice everyone to come to the Children's Society fête on Saturday – do you think you could manage it?'

Barbara thought swiftly. She had never patronised any local charities. Perhaps it was time she did.

'Yes, I'm sure I can,' she said as Mrs Pargetter-Wilson extracted a programme from the sheaf.

'It's two pounds – for such a good cause.'

'Excuse me, I'll just get my handbag,' Barbara said, quickly returning with two pound coins.

'Thank you, my dear. And you must come to one of our coffee mornings – you'd enjoy it. Perhaps,' and her visitor smiled archly, 'who knows, we may enlist your help? We could do with all the assistance we can get.'

This has been an extraordinary day, Barbara told herself.

'Thank you, I'll definitely consider it,' was all she said.

Mrs Pargetter-Wilson turned to go. 'Your garden is so pretty. I often admire it – a real cottage garden.'

'Thank you,' Barbara said, ruefully recognising the difference between her own cottage garden and the magnificently laid out grounds of the Lutyens house.

'Now don't forget,' said Mrs Pargetter-Wilson. 'We need your support on Saturday.' And she teetered off down the narrow path on her high heels, elegant legs almost too dainty for her somewhat top-heavy figure.

Barbara closed the door behind her yet again, and took the programme into the sitting room to scan. Yes, well, that might be enjoyable, and was undeniably in a good cause. She found herself feeling oddly exhilarated and remembered the bottle of wine she'd brought up from the cellar. She searched for a corkscrew, and with some difficulty managed to open it.

My second today, she thought, feeling very daring, and sat savouring her glass of wine, remembering again that nice man Bryan Payne and the visions he had conjured up for her of travel and adventure under Indian skies.

Walking on to Kirby Lodge, Mrs Pargetter-Wilson decided that she would call in after all – even though she knew the Whittakers were up to their eyes in wedding arrangements.

Anne and Eric were preparing for the wedding of their only daughter, Susannah, which was to take place at the end of June.

It was to be such a grand affair that they had been planning it for months. Eric Whittaker was a City tycoon and immensely wealthy, while Susannah was marrying into an aristocratic family. Not exactly royalty – but almost. Anne was a little woman with a North Country accent you could cut with a knife, one she would never lose, but she was well aware of the prestigious match her daughter was making and nothing but the best would do. It was difficult, Constance decided, to like people who appeared to have so much but she did like Anne, and Eric too. They were very good to the local community and always joined in every charity event. In fact, Anne was on several committees but had taken six months' leave of absence this year to ensure that Susannah's wedding was one to remember.

Constance walked up the winding drive and knocked on their door.

It was opened by Anne, her diminutive figure clad in a beautiful designer suit, blue eyes smiling at her visitor beneath hair turned prematurely white and cut close to her head.

'Constance! Lovely to see you, come on in.'

'No, I won't, dear,' she said. 'I only called to remind you about the Children's Society fête on Saturday. But I expect you'll be too busy to attend...'

'Yes, Con, sorry, I will have to miss it this year. Saturday's a special day for us. Susannah's cousin Jane is arriving from New York – you know my sister lives over there – and we're getting quite excited.'

They were interrupted by Susannah herself who came through from the back of the house. Her long ash blonde hair was tied back untidily, highlighting vivid blue eyes just like her mother's. She was dressed in riding clothes as usual. Susannah had always been mad about horses.

'Hello, Mrs Pargetter-Wilson.'

'Hello, my dear. I expect you're getting very excited, especially with your cousin coming.'

'Yes, I can't wait to see her.'

'Look,' Constance turned to go, 'I mustn't hold you up – I know you've a lot to do. If I can be of any help, do let me know. I'll leave you a programme.'

'Thanks,' Anne said, and watched her friend's stately progress down the drive. Constance, in the meantime, knew there would soon be a very generous cheque in the post for the Children's Society, and hoped for a wedding invitation sometime – she wouldn't miss that for the world.

Roll on Friday, the one evening she had all to herself... And Constance hummed a little tune, practically dancing her way back to The Cedars.

The next day Barbara went into Texbury to do her shopping, and at the end of the morning called into the travel agent's and picked up several brochures on India. Once home, having had her lunch, she relaxed, feet up on a stool, browsing through the information.

It seemed that February was a good time to go to India. How wonderful. It was such a bleak month here and to get away into the sunshine and warmth sounded just what the doctor ordered.

But next year ... such a long wait. Having made up her mind to go, Barbara was impatient. She would really like to be going this weekend and didn't relish the thought of waiting for months.

Still, there was a lot to organise apparently, it wasn't like taking a day trip across the Channel. Visa, jabs, passport in order – all the things that William once organised for her.

Oh, William, she thought. I wonder what you'd say if you knew what I'm about to do? I'm actually thinking of going to India at last.

But approve or disapprove William wasn't here to discuss it with and Barbara found herself wishing she had someone – anyone – with whom to share her momentous news.

Chapter Three

The following Saturday Barbara came out of the travel agent's on top of the world. She had done it! She had booked her trip to India. Now all that remained was to wait patiently. The jabs would come later but first she would have to go to town for her special visa.

'Hi, Barbara.' It was Viv McKay, walking along the High Street holding Ben's hand.

'Oh, Viv, how nice to see you. Hello, Ben.'

Barbara's eyes were shining like stars.

'What have you been up to?' Viv asked curiously.

'Oh, just something I've wanted to do for a long time.'

'Really? Look, why don't we go for a coffee at the Green Door and you can tell me all about it? Have you time?'

'All the time in the world.'

'Wish I had. See you there in ten minutes.'

They met up again and seated themselves at a corner table in the small cafe. 'Just coffee?' asked Viv.

'Yes, thanks. And this is on me incidentally. What about Ben?'

'Ice cream, please,' he said.

'No doubt about that then,' Viv said, smiling.

A young waitress who barely looked older than Ben himself took their order and went to the counter.

'Well, come on, don't keep me in suspense,' laughed Viv.

'I've booked my "passage to India",' Barbara said. 'Of course, I don't go until...' And then she saw the look of horror on Viv's face.

'India!'

'Oh, not for you, then?' Barbara laughed. 'I've wanted to go for years, but William, my husband–'

'Well, wild horses wouldn't drag *me* there. Still, if that's what turns you on.'

'February I'm going – got to have jabs, all that sort of thing, first. You know, Viv, I usually hate making decisions but this time it was easy. Having made up my mind, that was that. I'm so excited.'

'Well, good for you,' she said. 'It's never been a problem for me – making decisions – but I do find myself facing something pretty big at the moment and, to tell you the truth,

I'm really flummoxed.'

'Oh, Viv, that sounds serious. Want to tell me?'

Viv looked down at Ben as the waitress approached with their order, and shook her head slightly to show she did not want him to hear.

'Tell you what, are you doing anything tomorrow afternoon?'

'No,' Barbara said, knowing Sunday was always the worst day of the week for her.

'Well, my mother's coming over to lunch. Join us, if you like?'

'Oh, no thanks,' Barbara said swiftly. She had no desire to be too pushy and felt she'd be encroaching on a family event.

Viv obviously understood exactly what she was thinking.

'Well, Mum likes to take Ben for a walk after lunch, and George always has a nap after golf – if it's a nice day, we could sit in the garden later and have a cup of tea.'

'Come to me,' Barbara said impulsively. 'I'd like that. About three?'

'Thanks. I'd like another opinion although I know it's up to me in the end – only I can decide. So, tell me about this proposed trip. What exactly does it take in?'

They talked until they had finished their

coffee and Ben his ice cream, and then made their separate ways home.

'Will you be going to the fête this afternoon – I might take Ben?' Viv asked.

'Not sure,' Barbara said, knowing she would probably spend it tidying up the garden and polishing and dusting the house in honour of Viv's visit.

'See you tomorrow then. Come on, Ben.'

Barbara walked home on air. Not only had she a visitor to look forward to but she was actually going to India...

Satisfied with her efforts on Sunday, she had a quick lunch and surveyed the garden which she had worked on the best way she knew how. It did look good, early roses in bud and the wistaria just clinging on. Still there were the tulips and the wallflowers, and on the back wall the Albertine in bud – such a lot to look forward to.

When the doorbell rang her heart leapt, she was so unused to visitors. Viv stood on the doorstep in jeans and sweater carrying a small cake box.

'Hope you don't mind? My ma is a great cake maker – she brought me two and I've chosen the least fattening of them, an almond cake. If you like, we can have it with our tea.'

'Oh, thank you!' Barbara said. 'How kind. Come in.'

'Oh, isn't this pretty?' Viv said, looking around. 'It's so olde worlde.'

'Well, it's mostly my in-laws' furniture – I got rid of ours when we moved. I much preferred William's mother's stuff, she had such good taste and inherited some antiques from her parents' home. They're just small enough to fit in.'

'It's quite charming,' Viv said enthusiastically.

'We just washed over the walls. There was wallpaper everywhere, which made it look a little old-fashioned, so I colourwashed it all. At least, I should say, William did. He did everything around the house.' And Barbara's eyes clouded over.

Viv glanced at her swiftly.

'The garden! How pretty. Golly, I wish ours could look like that but we're neither of us gardeners and in any case...'

She didn't finish what she was saying. 'Go on through,' Barbara said, indicating the French windows beyond which she had placed chairs round a garden table. 'I've got the kettle on.'

Viv sank into a chair.

'Oh, what bliss!' she said. 'And to be

waited on.'

'I'll just cut the cake. I did buy one but, looking at this, I think I'll save it for another time. It looks delicious.'

'Yes, Ma's a dab hand at cake making. Wish I was. Still, I never seem to get the time to practise – or experiment rather. I think George is still hoping I'll come up trumps, but when you work–'

'Where do you work, Viv? And what do you do?'

'I work for Holland Bradshaw, the publishers.'

'Oh.' Barbara was impressed.

'I'm the assistant fiction editor,' Viv said, not without pride.

'How wonderful!'

'I suppose you'll be saying next that you could write a novel,' Viv said. 'Everyone does when you tell them you're in publishing.'

'No,' laughed Barbara, 'but I love books, that's why I became a librarian. Maybe I should try for a publishing job now the shop has closed?'

'Well, you'd have to travel up to town every day. That's where the best jobs are.'

'I wouldn't mind that. Give me something to do. But it must be difficult, juggling a job with looking after a home and a child. We never had any.'

'Are you sorry?'

'Yes, I am. Somehow they didn't come though – I – we did nothing to prevent them. I worked, so did William, yet when I look back on a twenty-year marriage I wonder where the time went. And now he's–'

'Well,' Viv said brightly, 'let me tell you about my little problem. What am I saying – *little* problem? It's a bloody – sorry – it's a big one.'

Barbara cut the cake and poured the tea.

'George, my husband, has been offered a good position in America – Florida to be exact – at a university there. He's an academic, you see, a mathematician.'

'Oh!' Barbara said, hopelessly impressed.

'Of course, I'm not denying it's a great opportunity and a step up.'

I can't bear it, Barbara thought. Just when I've found this new friend, she's about to leave.

'But,' Viv went on, 'you see, the problem is...'

Barbara waited.

'I don't want to go.'

'Oh, Viv!'

'Yes, I know it sounds awful, but honestly, Barbara, I just couldn't turn my life upside down to go and live in the United States.'

'So you mean George will have to refuse the job?'

'Oh, he won't do that,' Viv said. 'It's too good an opportunity to miss. Besides, he's raring to go.'

'But then what will you do?'

'You may well ask. I've already told him I really can't go and live over there – and nor do I want Ben to grow up in America. I want him to go to an English school, grow up an English boy. Do you see what I mean, Barbara?'

'But...' She was puzzled. 'Surely there has to be some sort of compromise? I mean–'

'You mean, I must give in and go to the States?'

'Well, he is Ben's dad and...'

'If George wants to uproot himself and sod off to America then I can't stop him. What I can do is stay here – with Ben,' Viv said flatly.

Barbara looked shocked.

'But then Ben would lose his dad.'

'He's lost his mum if George tries to take him,' Viv said carefully. 'I'm not going, Barbara. There's no way round it – it's too far to commute obviously.'

'What about your job?' Barbara asked.

'That's just it. I was lucky enough to get this position when we came down a year ago. I used to work for Haddington's in Manchester and then when I heard through the grapevine this job was going I applied and got it. I've been very lucky – it's not something I'd give up without a struggle. In fact, I don't intend to give it up full stop.' And Viv's mouth set in a belligerent line.

Barbara bit her lip. She could see both sides. Oh, thank God she had never had a decision like that to make.

'Do you love him – George?' she asked after a moment.

'Of course I do, and he loves me, but I don't love him enough to give up everything and live in the States for his sake.'

She turned troubled eyes to Barbara.

'Do you think I should?'

'Well, I'm a great believer in keeping a marriage together, especially when there's a child to consider.'

'But why can't George give in?'

'You call it giving in?'

'Well, yes, that's what it amounts to. That's what I mean – it's a really big decision.'

'Suppose,' Barbara said slowly, 'that he

takes up the offer and comes home, say, Christmas, Easter and summer holidays?'

'That's no way to live,' Viv scoffed. 'What kind of marriage is that? No, if he goes then he'd better not expect me to be waiting for him when he gets back.'

'Oh, Viv! Some people have to spend months – years apart in a marriage.'

'Not me,' she said. 'It's all or nothing with me.'

'Of course, years ago, there would have been no question about it,' Barbara said thoughtfully. 'I mean, where your husband went, you went too.'

'Ah, but times have changed,' Viv said, the light of battle in her eyes. 'Besides my boss is leaving next year – she'll be sixty and she's been there forever.'

'The fiction editor?'

'Yes, and I'm in line for her job. I know it backwards already and, what's more, she likes me. So...'

They sat saying nothing for a while, then Barbara spoke again.

'I expect George will give up the idea.'

'You think so? Well, I've got news for you. He is the most stubborn man I have ever met, and once he decides on something...'

'What – even where his wife and son are at

stake? I can't see it happening,' Barbara said slowly. 'Of course, I don't know your husband.'

'But you are sure everything will turn out all right in the end. And if I tell you that means he'll go–'

'–he'll have second thoughts when it comes to leaving you both, I'm sure of it,' Barbara said comfortingly.

'I wish I could believe you.'

'Of course, he could go alone for a spell to try it out? You could both try it out?'

'No.' Viv sounded adamant. 'Look, sorry, I'm casting a blight, aren't I? It's my problem and it's up to me to solve it. Let's leave it there.'

They sat silently for a moment.

'More tea?' asked Barbara, to lighten the atmosphere. Funny, she thought. From a widow's perspective any married woman was automatically in clover – when quite often from within a marriage the picture was anything but perfect.

Anne Whittaker was talking to her sister in Virginia on the telephone. Her eyes were filled with tears, her face pale.

'Oh, Felicity, I can hardly believe it! Poor Jane.'

She listened further, eyes staring sightlessly ahead. 'Oh, no, of course you can't ... no, never mind that. Would you like me to come over?... When is the funeral?'

She put her hand over the receiver as Susannah appeared dressed as usual in her jodhpurs and a cream polo neck sweater. 'Who is it?' she whispered, sensing something was wrong.

'Aunt Felicity,' Anne mouthed.

After further commiserations, she put down the phone and burst into tears.

'Oh, Mummy, what is it?' Susannah put an arm around her mother's heaving shoulders.

'It's Jane's fiancé – he's been killed in a riding accident.'

Susannah covered her face with her hands. 'Oh, no, how awful!'

'Yesterday it seems they were out riding – had gone to Virginia for the weekend – and he took a fence or hurdle or whatever, the horse refused to jump, threw Richard, and he was killed instantly. His neck was broken. Felicity flew from New York to Virginia immediately.'

'What a terrible thing to happen,' Susannah said, near to tears herself.

'So of course they won't be coming over for the wedding.'

'No, of course not. They were getting married themselves, weren't they?'

'In October, I understand. He was so young, only twenty-five, the same as Jane.'

Susannah shivered. 'Oh, I can't believe it.'

'Let's go and find your father, he'll be as shocked as I am,' Anne said, drying her tears and pulling herself together.

She took Susannah's arm in hers. 'Now we mustn't let this affect your wedding. It was a terrible accident but it mustn't detract from your big day. Oh, poor, poor Jane!'

'Well, the wedding is still six weeks away. Perhaps by then she could come. It might do her good to have a break. I haven't seen her since we were twelve, do you realise that? I know you've been over there with Daddy but I haven't and I was so looking forward to meeting Jane again.'

'No, darling, she won't feel like coming to a wedding of all occasions. The whole thing doesn't bear thinking of...'

Anne pushed open the door to Eric's study where she found him immersed in figures as usual.

'Sorry to disturb you, darling, but I've some rather sad news, I'm afraid.'

He turned in his chair, wide-eyed. 'What is it?'

'Flick's daughter Jane – her fiancé's been killed in a riding accident.'

'Oh, my God! How simply awful. The poor girl – how is she taking it?'

'Well, as you may imagine, Flick said they won't be able to come over for Susannah's wedding.'

'No, I daresay not. Does she want you to go over to New York?'

'No, I suggested it but she said not, and I can't say I'm sorry.'

'No,' he said gruffly. 'Poor old Flick. Well, you certainly must go over after the wedding or perhaps they could come over here for a break? What a terrible thing to happen.'

Susannah was standing by the open door, her blue eyes wide with shock.

He went over to her and put his arm around her shoulders. 'Now, don't go upsetting yourself,' he said. 'It was just a ghastly accident.'

'I know, Daddy, but I think I'll just go and ring Simon...'

As the door closed behind her, Eric turned to Anne, smiling wryly.

'Wants to reassure herself he's still breathing.' He smiled indulgently. 'Poor little thing, she can do without news like that just before her big day.'

Anne frowned. 'That's a selfish point of view, Eric. Imagine what Jane is feeling.'

'Perhaps it was a good thing they weren't already married.'

'I do hope it won't cast a cloud over our day,' Anne fretted.

'Of course it won't. The wedding's six weeks away. Plenty of time for Susannah to get used to the idea, though I expect she's disappointed Jane's not coming.'

'So am I. I was so looking forward to seeing my sister.'

'We'll take a trip to New York once the nuptials are over,' he said, in an effort to cheer her up.

'Oh, that would be lovely,' Anne said. Now that would be something else to plan, and there was nothing she enjoyed more than a project to organise.

When George woke up in Sunnyside, after his post-golf nap, the thoughts came crowding in again. They wouldn't go away. They were with him all the time – thoughts of Viv and Ben and a new life for them all in the States.

He was surprised how deeply Viv had dug herself in over it – after all, he had thought she would be delighted. He hadn't expected such a draconian reaction to his news. He stretched himself and shrugged. But there was no question about it, he was going to take that job. And unless he was very much mistaken, Viv and Ben were going with him.

Of course, he thought indulgently, it had been a shock. Uprooting themselves would be a bind, although he was very keen on the move, and knew Viv was adaptable. A sensible girl, Viv, called a spade a spade. But he had not expected such a vehement response, he had to admit. Ben would love it – such an opportunity – and for him too. Who knew where he would end up? Opportunities and chances in the New World. He hummed to himself, 'New York, New York'. Yes, he could make it there and his wife would come round. Anyway, he hadn't told her this but he had already written officially accepting the job. No two ways about it. He hadn't foreseen this opposition, that was the trouble.

When his mother-in-law returned from her walk with Ben, George had already got the kettle on for tea.

'Nice walk, Pam?' he said. He got on well with his mother-in-law.

'Yes, it was lovely. We walked over the

common, saw some horse riders, didn't we, Ben?'

He was already sitting down with his Lego on the floor.

'Did Viv tell you about...'

She looked meaningfully down at the child.

'Yes, she did, George.'

He made the tea, priding himself on being so domesticated.

'What do you think?' he murmured, careful not to attract Ben's attention.

'I'm all for it, but you'll have to talk Viv round.'

'Oh, she'll give in,' he said confidently. 'She's just got to get used to the idea.'

'Here, let me do that,' said Pam, getting down cups and saucers and tea plates and the second cake, with none of the fuss and commotion he would have made.

Having laid the table she sat opposite him. 'Does – er – he know?'

'No, we haven't mentioned it yet owing to the – er–'

'Yes, I see. Well, you'll have to soon, won't you? When are you due to...'

'A.s.a.p.'

Ben got fed up with this cryptic conversation.

'I'm going out into the garden,' he said, and saw with relief his mother coming through the back gate.

'Oh, Ben,' she greeted him. 'Nice walk?'

'Brilliant,' he said. 'I'm making a JCB.'

'Lovely,' she said, without a clue what it was. 'Like some tea?'

'No, thanks, I'm busy. And Dad and Gran keep going all funny and not finishing what they're saying. It's more peaceful out here.'

'Fair enough,' said Viv, her heart sinking. She knew without asking just what they'd been talking about.

Having cleared away the tea things and put them in the dishwasher, Barbara returned to the garden to sit and contemplate Viv's problem. It seemed so unreal to her. She couldn't imagine such a situation. There they were, a young family, all their future before them, and Viv had decided not to accompany her husband on his new job. Surely it was a wife's duty to be with her husband? She could not imagine herself in such a situation. If it had been William, she would have followed him to the ends of the earth – well, almost. She certainly would not have said, 'I'm not coming with you.' Husbands and wives had a duty towards each other, hadn't they? Of course, she herself was not a feminist or whatever they called themselves these days – but where would it all lead?

And that dear little boy, what would happen to him? You read of tug-of-war struggles involving children – how could Viv do such a thing? And yet she said she loved him...

It had to be the generation gap. She simply could not get her head around it. Viv was so nice – a warm, kind person – someone you could talk to. She'd felt they really had something in common, but had they?

Barbara couldn't even begin to think like Viv. When you had a good man like that, how could you let him go? Life could be so lonely without a husband – or partner which was what they called them today. That was something else she didn't go along with. She knew things were changing, but even so.

Oh, it was all very worrying.

She went indoors and picked up her Indian brochures again. What would Viv do if she kept to her word and didn't go? It was tantamount to breaking up her marriage, wasn't it?

Chapter Four

Viv stood in the kitchen with arms folded.

'I cannot believe,' she said to George, 'that you have actually *accepted* that job without consulting me.'

'I did consult you.' He dug in his heels, red-faced with shame.

'And I said no. I had no intention of coming with you.'

'And you still feel like that?' His voice was cold.

'Of course I do. I don't make idle threats.' Her nostrils were dilating, breath coming harshly.

'So it's stalemate,' he said.

'What's that supposed to mean?'

'That I intend to go, Viv. Look, this is the chance of a lifetime. I'm thirty-nine, I may never get another opportunity like this.'

'So you said. Well, if you don't mind leaving your wife and child behind–'

'But for God's sake, Viv, you can come with me!'

'You know I have no intention of doing

that,' she said coldly.

He stared at her for a long time. 'I had no idea you could be so hard.'

'And I had no idea that you could take a new job without considering me and my feelings.'

There was a short silence which she broke.

'Has it ever occurred to you, George, that I have a life, too? I have a job, a very good job, with a real chance of promotion. Are you telling me you've given no thought to that – to my professional future?'

'And you'd put *that* before me and our family? I've always thought it was my duty to take care of you and Ben the best way I know how...'

'Oh, I see, you Tarzan – me Jane,' she sneered.

'I don't know you like this,' he said. 'After all, we moved south when I had to relocate.'

'Oh, puh-lease, this is entirely different. You chose to apply for a job in another country and accepted it knowing I had absolutely no intention of moving.'

'I seem to have got you all wrong, Viv.'

'You certainly have,' she snorted.

It was their first really big row and upstairs Ben tucked himself further down under the duvet and pulled it over his head.

Over the next couple of weeks he heard further snippets from time to time and put things together for himself. He knew that his father taught sums for a living which was odd when he was no good at them himself! Then came the day when they told him that Daddy was going away across the sea to the United States of America to teach people there, and perhaps later in the summer Ben and Mum would go over for a holiday. His father was going to lecture at a university in Florida. They told him all about Florida, what was there, the dolphins and the sea and Cape Canaveral... It sounded great but when the time came for his father to leave he was miserable and had to fight not to cry. It was the same for his mummy, he knew, though she never said a word about how she was feeling or even that she'd miss not having Dad around the house, which was odd because she sat for hours the first few evenings not saying anything and he caught her wearing one of Dad's old tee-shirts in bed.

They went to tea at Auntie Barbara's. It was a Saturday and it seemed funny not to have Dad at home then. Auntie Barbara let him play in the garden and feed the fish in the little pond.

'Oh, I am sorry!' she said to Viv as she put the kettle on.

Her friend dried her eyes. 'I can't believe he's really gone,' she said. 'Right up to the last minute, I didn't think he'd go.'

'How was he?'

'Well, upset at leaving Ben behind mainly, but you could see he was excited about it all underneath.'

She sniffed and blew her nose.

'I've compromised,' she said. 'Against my better judgement, I have to say. I'm taking Ben over for a fortnight's holiday just before he goes back to school – I suppose that's fair enough. But it won't make any difference to how I feel. If George thinks that it will he's very much mistaken,' she added darkly.

Life changed a lot for Ben after that. For a start, Grandma Haley came to stay quite a bit. He liked his Grandma Haley. She was nice, and she understood Lego, and had time for him. She also took him to school sometimes and collected him.

One day he heard her say, 'You're making a big mistake, Viv, mark my words. You're being selfish and there'll be plenty of other women over there...' Then Mum gave a warning frown and she went quiet.

Ben shot his mother a quick look. He

hadn't realised grown ups could make mistakes.

It was the beginning of June, and life was certainly hectic at Kirby Lodge. There was great excitement throughout this very special month, and today William the chauffeur was driving Susannah and Anne Whittaker up to town.

In the car Anne consulted a quite lengthy list, glancing occasionally at Susannah and approving what she saw. It was a change to get the girl out of riding clothes. Still, once she was married both she and Simon would probably spend their lives in the stables or on the hunting field.

Her daughter looked lovely, fair hair tied back, blue eyes tranquil, as happy and contented as a lark. As well she might, thought Anne, considering the man she was going to marry. Simon was a good catch by anyone's standards.

'We'll make our first call at Hélène's,' she said, Hélène being the very fashionable young Hungarian designer who was making the wedding dress. If she was good enough for a royal princess, she was the designer who would best serve a Whittaker bride-to-be.

'I hate fittings,' Susannah said, her full mouth pursed in a pout.

'Now, darling, it can't be helped. The more fittings you have, the better the dress. And we do want you to show off that lovely figure of yours.'

Anne consulted her list. 'Then to Rayne and Ferragamo...'

'But, Mummy, I prefer Jimmy Choo,' Susannah protested.

'Very well, dear, then Versace and Dior. We won't have time for a lot more today, I shall be exhausted after lunch. I'll ask William to pick us up at three. Oh, and a quick call into Harrods.'

'Mummy, no one in their right mind goes to Harrods any more.'

'Very well then, Harvey Nicks,' Anne said.

This, she knew, would be the first of many such trips to London before they finally completed Susannah's trousseau.

They stopped in Fulham where Hélène Shranov lived and were there for over an hour. Tears came to Anne's eyes as she finally looked at her daughter's reflection in the full-length mirror.

The dress was a dream: ivory silk, classical in design, looking as if it had been moulded on to her perfect figure. There was nothing outré about it. The magic lay in the cut as it hugged her breasts and waist and gently swirled around her ankles. Not too low-cut, with long tight sleeves, it was a classic. Anne was aiming to please Simon's family with the tastefulness and restraint of the bride's triumphal appearance.

'You don't think it should be just a little lower?' Susannah asked, fingering the neckline as it circled her smooth neck.

'No, darling,' Anne said firmly, eyeing the miraculous darts Hélène had employed in order to skim the figure while enhancing it.

Later Anne watched her daughter as she tried on shoes: featherlight, of softest ivory satin, with the most ridiculous high heels. Was it possible she herself had ever worn such shoes?

But they had, of course, in her day too, when they wanted to look their absolute best. She didn't think she could wear them now. And the materials they used: rhinestone straps, silks and satin, crocodile skin for handbags. Which reminded her, Susannah needed bags. They'd better go to Asprey for those, her father would probably want to buy them for her.

There was so much to do and her list was still lengthy, even though she had spent most of the morning ticking items off.

'Let's go to lunch,' she said. 'I'm quite hungry – are you?'

'Yes, starving,' Susannah said, and slipping her arm under her mother's made for the trendy little restaurant they liked just off Knightsbridge.

They arrived home soon after four, exhausted from their efforts. William unpacked the boot and carried in the elegantly wrapped packages. As they walked into the hall, Eric came towards them.

'Had a good day?' he asked, kissing them both. 'There's an e-mail for you, Anne, from Felicity.'

'Oh!' And she hurried eagerly in search of it. They heard her little shriek of delight and saw her emerge with a wide smile on her face.

'How wonderful – Jane is coming over for the wedding!'

'Oh, Mummy! That's great! Is Aunt Felicity coming with her?'

'No, she's coming on her own – your aunt thinks it might be just what she needs to take her out of herself.' Anne frowned suddenly. 'Oh, I do hope so. I hope the sight of you in your wedding dress won't throw her ... you should see her, Eric. She'll be the most beautiful bride you ever saw.'

'I've always said so,' Eric Whittaker said calmly. 'Simon is a very lucky young man.'

'Oh, Daddy!' Susannah said, and went upstairs to unpack her purchases. She adored her father.

Two weeks later Jane arrived. There was just a fortnight to go before the wedding and a welcome party had been arranged for the evening after her arrival at which she was to meet the family again and many of the wedding guests.

Susannah drove with William to Heathrow to pick her up, half her mind on the forthcoming wedding and the other half on the cousin she scarcely remembered in the flesh although there had been many family photographs exchanged over the years. Susannah remembered her as quite a serious girl. It was known that she was very clever, but that horse riding was her passion.

At the arrivals gate Susannah recognised her long before William did: a neat little figure in jeans and polo neck sweater, a cloud of dark hair about her shoulders and great dark eyes turned enquiringly in Susannah's direction.

'Oh, Jane, how lovely to see you!' She threw her arms around her cousin.

'Susannah – why, it's been years. Oh, you look so pretty.'

That soft American accent, southern in tone, was strangely charming, Susannah felt.

'Did you have a good flight?' she asked.

'Yes, uneventful,' Jane said, but she still hadn't smiled. How sad for her, Susannah thought, remembering what she had so recently been through. 'Well, let's take your luggage and William will drive us home.'

We shall have to make every effort to give her a good time, Susannah decided. Perhaps it wasn't such a good idea for her to come after all. How could she fail to think of her own wedding and what might have been?

'It is so nice to be here,' Jane said in a composed voice as William stowed her luggage in the boot.

In the back of the car, sitting beside her, Susannah stole sidelong glances at her cousin, seeing the pale magnolia skin, so typical of certain Americans, the thick fall of soft dark hair which made a perfect frame for her face. She was smaller than Susannah remembered; she herself felt outsize by comparison though she was slim by most people's standards. Jane stared out of the window at the scenery, saying little, and

Susannah told herself her cousin had just had a long flight and was probably jet lagged.

'I expect you'll want a long sleep when you get home, but tomorrow we're holding a welcome party for you – we know you Americans always do these things so well and we want you to feel at home here. Mummy and Daddy are looking so forward to seeing you again.'

She wanted to say how sorry she was about the death of Jane's fiancé, but thought better of it – she had no desire to rake it all up again. There would be time enough for that later.

'Oh!' Jane whispered softly when they drew up at Birch Common and drove towards Kirby Lodge. William negotiated the switch that opened the gates to the drive. 'It hasn't changed a bit! It's just as lovely as ever. Do you know, I can remember it from way back, when I was small.'

Her face was more animated now, and the lovely dark eyes shone.

That's better, thought Susannah. 'How old were you when you came over last?'

'About eleven or twelve, I guess,' Jane said. 'It hasn't changed at all. I'm glad.'

Anne and Eric were waiting at the top of

the steps and came down to greet her. Anne put her arms around her niece, holding her close, while Eric smiled a welcome.

'Welcome to Kirby Lodge, my dear,' Anne said, 'we are delighted to see you.' Eric kissed her lightly on the cheek.

How small and dainty she was, Anne thought. She had forgotten what a neat little thing Jane was, and so frail-looking now, almost pathetic. Anne felt she wanted to mother her and feed her up. By comparison Susannah looked the picture of health. Oh, she did hope she had done right in persuading Felicity that it would be a good idea for Jane to visit now.

'Come along and Susannah will show you to your room,' she said. 'This way.'

Up the steps and into the beautiful hall of the old house, so distinctive with its stone flooring and beautiful paintings adorning the walls. At the far end, past the horseshoe staircase, was a magnificent stained glass window, which even now reflected coloured images that danced on the floor, and the great centrepiece of flowers on the table.

'How beautiful it all is,' Jane whispered half to herself. 'Oh, Susannah, you are so lucky.'

Hastily, Susannah gave her a brilliant

smile – she was not her mother's daughter for nothing and had learned diplomacy at a very early age.

'I know,' she laughed. 'We are terribly spoiled. Come on, this way. Edith will bring your things up. She's been with us forever – I don't know if you remember her?'

Up the thickly carpeted stairs with their old brass rods to the upper hall where at the end of the wide landing Susannah showed Jane to her room.

'There!' she said, not without a sense of pride, as she revealed the panelled room with its yellow and cream decor, heavy curtains which spilled over on to the floor, antique furniture and a door leading to the most modern of bathrooms.

'This is smashing,' said Jane, not even attempting to hide her astonishment.

Susannah laughed. 'Yes, I expect we have improved our bathrooms since you were here last. We've learned a thing or two since then.' And she pointed out the wide deep bath and the shower where there was every attachment a girl could want.

'I'll leave you to settle in,' she said. 'I'm just across the hall from you on the right if there's anything you want, but I expect you'd like to be alone for a while. Do have a little sleep if you'd like and come down when you're ready. Edith will be along presently.'

Jane turned her huge dark eyes to Susannah, her head slightly tilted to one side.

'You're very kind,' she said. 'I was so looking forward to coming but...' She caught her breath, unable to continue.

Susannah crossed swiftly over to her and kissed her on the cheek.

'Don't worry about a thing,' she said. 'We want you to enjoy your stay.'

When the door closed behind her, Jane flopped on to the bed face down and wept, her clenched fists pummelling the pillows.

'How was she?' Anne asked anxiously when Susannah joined her parents.

'She looked exhausted. I left her to rest. I don't think she knows if she's on her head or her heels.'

'I'm not so sure that it was a good idea for her to come. Imagine her feelings when she sees you and Simon at the wedding ceremony.'

'Look, Mummy, she wouldn't have come unless she'd wanted to. I expect she felt so lost at home almost anything would be a welcome break.'

'Daddy and I have decided to spend a

week in town after you leave for your honeymoon. We've organised a little party for her at the Ritz and we've already asked some of her other cousins. Uncle Henry's boys will be there, and we'll take her out to dinner at some of London's best restaurants and to see one or two shows.'

'Oh, I'm quite envious!' laughed Susannah. 'Mummy, you are sweet. I just know you'll do all you can for her. It really is sad, isn't it? Just when I'm feeling on top of the world, too.'

She glanced at her watch. 'I think I'll just nip over to Simon's. There's time before dinner, isn't there?'

'It's at eight,' Anne said, and frowned. 'Darling, you're not driving up to Henley now, are you? It's half-past four.'

'No problem,' Susannah said, 'if I hurry. I want to see Simon about something before the party tomorrow.'

'Couldn't you phone him?'

'No.' Susannah grinned. 'I want to see him, OK? Jane will sleep for an hour or two, I expect, I shall be back by then. 'Bye for now.' She rushed out and Anne heard her MG start up and race round the common before making for the A40.

Simon Rawnsley was emerging from the stables when he heard the distinctive sound of Susannah's car and a smile instantly lit up his face.

He was a good-looking young man, over six foot tall, fair-haired and with deep grey eyes. His marrying Susannah Whittaker had been almost a foregone conclusion for they had known each other since they were in their teens, having met at the local riding stables where his mother had insisted he took full tuition although they kept a good stable of their own at Fulford Manor.

With Simon being just eighteen months older than Susannah, they had become fast friends when they first met, their joint interests being the countryside and riding. They were inseparable and never happier than in each other's company.

The only son of Lord Rawnsley, Simon was heir to the vast family estate, miraculously held on to through the hard post-war years, mainly thanks to Lady Rawnsley's efforts to keep the house open to the public and several other innovations of hers, such as a plant centre and farm provisions shop, which made it a year-round destination for visitors. She was, apart from anything else, an astute businesswoman.

She was delighted by her son's engagement to Susannah, knowing that the Whittakers had no dark secrets and, more importantly, that the bride would arrive with an excellent dowry. Eric Whittaker was a bluff, straight-talking tycoon, but a gentleman for all that.

Susannah parked her car and went over to Simon. He was never surprised to see her at any time of the day for she was a creature of impulse and followed her instincts. He took her in his arms and kissed her.

'Mmmm,' she said. 'It was worth coming over just for that.'

They stood close together, his arm around her shoulders.

'I can only stay a minute, actually,' Susannah said. 'Jane has arrived. We went to the airport to pick her up.'

'Oh, your cousin from the States?'

'Yes, poor thing, I feel so sorry for her. But I just wanted to make sure that everything was all right for tomorrow evening?'

'In what way?'

'Well, that you'll be bringing lots of your friends?'

'Some may arrive later. One or two of them actually work, darling.'

'Particularly Gil,' she went on, unperturbed.

78

'Oh, yes, he'll be there.'

Gilroy Maclean was Simon's best friend and was to be his best man.

'Oh, that's fine then. I have a feeling that Jane might like Gil. Of course, it's early days yet for her.'

'Darling, surely you have no time for matchmaking – what's she like anyway?'

'Oh, pretty, quiet – not surprisingly – a little bit lost.'

'I mean, what's she really like? There's no shortage of pretty girls around Gil, as you know.'

'Well, do ask him not to bring one, won't you? I'd like him to be free to partner Jane at the disco. I mean, I just don't want her to be left out of anything. I feel sort of responsible for her.'

They were walking towards the house now.

'Is your mother in?'

'Yes, she is.

'I'll just have a word with her. Darling, are you getting excited? It's only two more weeks and then...'

She looked up at him with starry eyes.

He bent and kissed her.

It was a glorious summer evening, June at its best, and the grounds of Kirby Lodge were alive with young people.

Music came from the rose garden, soft romantic strings, while in a corner of the meadow a rock group was assembling itself. A barbecue had been laid on another lawn, and the smell had begun to fill the air with tempting aromas. All the girls seemed to be in various stages of undress, or so thought Anne Whittaker, aware that her own daughter was the fairest of them all with her long blonde hair and the particular radiance of a bride-to-be. All the girls were attractive and the young men handsome, or so it seemed on this magical evening. Susannah wore palest blue with thin diamante straps over the shoulders. Lots of the girls were in similar pastels, but it was Jane who took Anne's eye.

She frowned slightly. There had surely been no need to dress in quite such a drab colour, for the dress was dark brown, a chocolate colour, brief, and so beautifully cut that it hugged her slender figure and showed off her excellent legs. Almost like a moth, Anne thought, she stood out for her very difference. Around her creamy throat she wore a thin gold chain with a single diamond which shone as it caught the sunlight. But it was her hair, that cloud of soft dark hair falling in waves and curls, so obviously natural, that marked her out with so many blondes about.

Many girls wore very low-cut dresses which left nothing to the imagination. Such was the fashion, it made them look like frivolous butterflies, but there was no denying the attractions of Jane's figure. That slightly forbidding dress seemed to be sculpted on to her.

Not knowing why, Anne bit her lip as she passed among the crowd, acknowledging them all.

Seeing a young man, broader and taller than most, she frowned. Dennis Pargetter-Wilson. She rather wished he hadn't come but one had to ask the neighbours even if one didn't quite approve of them. Dennis was such a silly young man, but his mother Constance was a good friend.

'Good evening, Mrs Whittaker,' he said. 'Lovely party.'

'Thank you. There'll be something to eat presently.' And, smiling cordially, Anne walked on.

A trio emerged from the house, Susannah, Simon and Gilroy Maclean, standing at the top of the steps for a moment, then walking slowly down and mingling with the guests.

Susannah swiftly moved over to where Jane stood, a lone figure almost merging with the shadows of the tree she stood under, holding a glass of champagne.

Going up to her, Susannah took her hand. 'Jane, dear.'

She turned her head and looked at her cousin, then at the two men with her.

'Jane, I'd like you to meet my fiancé Simon – and this is Gilroy Maclean who is to be our best man.'

Both men stared at Jane approvingly but it was Simon, looking down into those big dark eyes fringed as they were by the longest lashes he had ever seen, who felt as though he had been kicked in the stomach.

He found himself literally speechless as Gil held out his hand and took Jane's.

'Welcome to the UK,' he said.

But Simon and Jane held each other's gaze for what seemed forever as Susannah, her heart beating unusually fast, forced a smile.

'Hello, Simon,' Jane said at length, in that soft low voice of hers which sounded so musical in the midst of so many strident tones.

'How do you do?' he said, finding his own voice at last.

'Let's circulate, shall we?' Susannah said,

almost pleadingly.

'Of course,' Jane said gently and moved ahead, followed by Susannah, Gil and finally Simon.

Chapter Five

There was a desultory buzz of conversation as the ladies awaited the president of their branch of the Children's Society. Among them sat Barbara Cooper on her first visit to the volunteer section of the society.

She had made up her mind to do voluntary work for the rest of the year, see how she got on. Then there'd be her trip to India at the beginning of February, and plenty of time after that to look around for another proper job. She couldn't afford not to have a salaried job indefinitely, she needed money to live on, but at least the house was her own, and she was in no immediate need.

There was a small burst of applause as Constance Pargetter-Wilson appeared. It seemed nothing would go smoothly until she was in charge, whereas somehow with her in the chair everything would be taken care of.

She was a large lady in every sense, extremely well turned out in her favourite black, this time a silk blouse and fine wool skirt worn with her real pearl earrings which she wore constantly. Her straight hair, almost black in colour, was pulled back into a chignon, she had a smooth oval face with magnificent dark eyes, but her finest features were her elegant legs and finely turned ankles which seemed out of proportion to the rest of her. Several women from their vantage point below the platform tried to guess what happened to those legs higher up beneath the severe black skirt. There was no way of knowing if the rest of them was as good.

'Good afternoon, ladies,' Constance began, and there was an answering murmur.

'So good of you to come when I know most of you have lots to do and children to pick up from school. However, just one or two salient points. You will be pleased to know that we made a grand total of two hundred and sixty-eight pounds at the fête.' There was a burst of applause which went on until she put up her hand for quiet.

'Yes, well, you all worked very hard. And now I shall run through the business in hand as quickly as I can.'

She spent the next quarter of an hour dealing with past activities before coming to the point of this meeting.

'I know you will welcome three new volunteers–' she glanced down at the paper in her hand, '–Rose Findlay, Amanda Greenway and Barbara Cooper. Will those ladies stand up, please?'

Barbara had never felt so embarrassed. Everyone applauded until they sheepishly sat down again.

'Now, if they will come and see me at the end of the meeting, we will discuss what they are going to do – and very grateful we will be for it, won't we, ladies?'

Everyone apparently agreed, and at the end of the meeting Barbara found herself before the table where Constance sat with two or three other committee members. Having volunteered to work in the charity shop for two mornings a week, Barbara received her instructions. She was to report to the shop in Texbury at nine a.m. where she would work until one in the afternoon. The manageress would show her what to do. That she had already worked in a bookshop seemed to stand her in good stead and, flushed with her successful debut as a charity worker, she made her way home.

There was quite a lift in her spirits with the knowledge that she had something useful to do. She polished the furniture and scoured the bathroom with more enthusiasm than she had felt for a long time.

The next morning at nine, she walked into Texbury. After tapping on the locked door of the charity shop, she was let in by the manageress, Gladys Coke.

'Oh, am I glad to see you,' she said. 'Annie hasn't turned up yet and I've a mountain out there as big as Everest. Come through this way.'

There was the slightly acrid smell of used clothing in the airless storeroom at the back of the shop until Gladys opened a window.

'Have to watch it,' she said. 'They're supposed to be coming to put mesh over the windows. Still...' And she began to spray everywhere with room freshener until Barbara found herself choking. She received a vigorous thump on the back.

'Now, you've not done this before, have you?' said Gladys. 'I would have liked you to go on the till – I believe you're used to working one?'

'Well, I don't know about this one,' Barbara said, thinking of the up-to-date model which was not in the least like the one in the bookshop.

'Oh, you'll manage that all right. But in the meantime, until Doris gets here, you'll have to help me sort this lot out. Hang your own coat up there and stuff your handbag in the drawer. We keep it locked, you never know...'

Barbara did as she was told, and eyed the mountain of clothes and the stack of bin bags nervously.

'Now, I'll sort and when we've got some sort of a pile you can begin marking. There's a list on the wall with prices for ladies' skirts, blouses and trousers. All the men's stuff goes over in this pile. If you see anything that is obviously rubbish, torn stuff or dirty clothes, put it in bin bags. You'd be surprised what some people bring in. They use this as a rubbish dump – saves them a journey. Oh, hello, Annie. I thought you'd never get here. This is Barbara, come to help us. Oh, and there *you* are, Doris...'

Barbara had never worked so hard in her life, but they were all so friendly and anxious to put her right: 'Not just the amount on the till but the stock number ... like men's trousers, number four. Ladies' skirts, number two. Blouses, number five...'

I'll never remember it all, she thought. To think I've been wasting so much time at home.

'Now we open at nine-thirty so you'll have

a chance to do a bit of sorting first. Oh, and flick round with that feather duster you'll find in the drawer under the counter. When we've tackled this pile you can go on the till. If you don't understand anything, ask Doris.'

The back room was hot and stuffy and full of bin bags. Clothes hung from rails overhead: men's ironed shirts, ladies' blouses and tee-shirts, cardigans, rows of handbags. After ten minutes of sorting Gladys withdrew from one bag a crumpled heavy white silk dress.

'Ah, Balmain,' she said. 'Always look at the label. This is a model, see, separately priced. Look on the wall if you're in any doubt or ask one of us.' She held it out in front of her. Probably from the seventies, Barbara thought. It was knee-length, beautifully made, with padded shoulders. 'Could do with a press,' Gladys said, hanging it carefully on a hanger. 'Labels are important. Jaeger, Windsmoor, Viyella ... we ask more for those.' She hung the dress on the wall for pressing. 'Here's the steam press,' she said. 'Nothing to it. When you've a spare moment you can do that too. This way!' And she marched out of the storeroom and into the shop. 'Doris,' she said to the woman who

89

stood by the till, dusting and putting things to rights, 'stop fiddling with those CDs and give me a hand. What are we going to put by the door today?'

Doris looked terribly worried, obviously in awe of Gladys.

'Um...'

'On this bit here, by the wall, we usually hang something special. Passers-by can see it through the glass door. I know,' said Gladys, having a brainwave, 'them brides-maid's dresses.'

She almost ran back to the storeroom, flinging over her shoulder 'Come on!' to Barbara.

She found herself running too. 'Get that box down,' Gladys commanded. 'There's the ladder.'

Barbara dutifully climbed it. 'This one?' Gladys nodded impatiently.

Once on the floor the box was opened to reveal not one but three matching brides-maid's outfits.

'Oh!' Barbara murmured, privately appalled. Who on earth would have wanted to be attended by a trio of goldfish?

Bright orange satin, tightly waisted with very full skirts on which were tied many bows of the same orange satin, they had

90

white lacy puff sleeves and white lace fichus at the neck. They were all the same size, a ten, Barbara thought. Gladys viewed them with pride.

'Now,' she said triumphantly, 'we'll hang those by the door, that'll get 'em in.'

Draping them over her arms, she advanced on the wall by the door and hung them on three hooks, looking like strange variants on plaster ducks in a television period drama. 'Labels, Doris!' she called. 'Fifteen quid each, forty for the three.'

Doris duly brought over the label she'd written and Gladys handed the stapling gun to Barbara. 'Staple them on the edge of the sleeve,' she said impatiently, which Barbara did clumsily, not having used one before. 'Now don't they look a treat?' said Gladys, standing back to admire them. Then she glanced at her watch.

'Doris – the door!' she commanded, and Doris flew to the door and unlocked it.

Coffee was offered to Barbara several times, instant tasteless stuff: 'And there's biscuits over there in the tin.'

She couldn't have eaten anything to save her life.

At ten o'clock, Gladys suggested that the door should stay open – 'It's warm enough, and fresh air will keep us on our toes' – while Barbara studied the till and its intricacies.

Well-dressed women sidled in and flicked through the clothes with expert hands. There was always someone looking through the books, and once she saw a young woman with a pushchair stuff a shirt beneath the child sitting in it, unaware that she was being watched. Stunned at this effrontery Barbara watched open-mouthed as the girl left the shop, her face as innocent as a baby's.

At almost eleven Gladys emerged with a mauve jacket over her arm and a hanger in her hand. The jacket was stiff with gilt braiding and buttons all the way up the sleeves.

'What about that?' she said with triumph. 'Versaze!'

'Golly,' Doris said dutifully.

Barbara left the counter and walked over to inspect it, seeing the label 'VERSACE'.

'What's it say?' Gladys demanded, suspecting she'd got it wrong.

'Versace,' Barbara replied.

'Oh, I've no time for these foreign names,' Gladys said, looking idly round towards the special wall by the door and suddenly freezing.

They all did, following her gaze.

There were just two bridesmaids' dresses hanging there. Barbara and Doris looked at each other in consternation.

'Did you sell one?' Gladys asked accusingly.

They shook their heads, feeling as guilty as hell. It was worse than being at school.

'Annie!' Gladys yelled. She came running out of the storeroom, looking terrified. 'Did you sell one of them bridesmaid's dresses?'

'No, Gladys,' she said. She hadn't left the storeroom all morning.

'Someone's nicked one,' Gladys said gloomily, and gave a great sigh.

'Now I've told you before to keep your eyes open. It only takes a second for those thieving buggers to put their hands round the door.'

Barbara wanted to say, Why leave them so close to it then? But she didn't. She didn't dare.

'Label,' Gladys commanded. 'Twenty-five quid.' And this time had the sense to put the Versace jacket on one of the stands in a prominent place.

Barbara found herself outside the shop at one-fifteen. It was like stepping into another world, and she took great breaths of clean fresh air.

She wouldn't shop on her way home, she decided. All she wanted to do was get back and have a bath. But she found herself looking forward to the next session on Thursday nevertheless.

At Kirby Lodge, Susannah and Simon, who had stayed overnight, were in the paddock.

'I thought we'd have time for a brisk canter before you go,' she said, 'and then I really must get cracking. There's so much to do and Mummy needs a hand.'

By the stable door, Simon stood examining Hindsight's fetlocks. Hearing footsteps, Susannah turned. Frowning slightly at first, she collected herself and greeted her cousin warmly.

'Hi there, Jane. I thought you might want to sleep late.'

'No, I've been up some time.'

Simon looked up briefly. 'Hello, Jane.'

She wore jeans and a white sweater – obviously she had not come out for a ride. Her hair was casually arranged in a thick plait, but even so wild tendrils had escaped here and there. Jane's hair had a will of its own, Susannah thought, and although her face was pale, her dark eyes were burning with life.

'Look, would you like a ride or...' Susannah was interrupted by the ringing of her mobile phone.

'Oh, excuse me... Yes, Mummy... Oh, not now? Why have they come so early?... No – no, I know you can't. All right, I'll be over.'

'Sorry about that,' she said, switching off and slipping the mobile into her pocket. 'I've got to go back to the house. It won't take long – just something that needs sorting out.'

She turned to go then thought better of it. 'Jane, if you'd care to ride, Simon will help you. She could take Missy,' she said to him. 'See you later.'

'Oh, but...'

Jane stood uncertainly with her head hanging down. Unsure how to treat her, Simon stood watching her.

'Look,' he said finally, 'I know this is awkward for you – it must have been ghastly these last few weeks – but you're welcome to join me. I'm not going far, just exercising Hindsight.'

Jane shook her head, then raised those great dark eyes to his.

'I haven't been on a horse since Richard died.'

'But that's–'

'Yes, long enough. I just can't bring myself to.'

'I understand from Susannah and her mother that you are a born horsewoman.'

She looked ashen-faced.

'Don't you know the principle of getting right back on again, not wasting time, otherwise...'

'Yes, I know all that. But sorry, Simon. I just can't.'

'Would you if I gave you a helping hand?'

She looked down. 'I'm not properly dressed.'

'That's doesn't matter. Look, I'll get Missy. She's very sweet and docile.'

Without further ado, he went into the stables and led out the mare. Jane patted her. 'She's lovely.'

'And gentle. She was a present to Susannah on her twenty-first birthday.'

'Lucky Susannah.'

Jane stood eyeing the horse as Simon went to saddle her up.

'Don't, please,' she told him. 'I couldn't possibly...'

He disappeared into the stables and came out with a riding hat.

'Here, shove this on,' he said. 'I'm not

going to take no for an answer.'

She found herself strapping the hat under her chin but still made no move as Missy stood quietly beside her.

'Come on,' he said, holding two clasped hands below her.

Almost mesmerised, she stepped into the hands and he swung her on to Missy. Jane found herself taking the reins, her eyes bright with excitement, her body stiff with trepidation.

In a moment Simon was astride Hindsight, waiting to move.

'You first.' He grinned, waiting for her to set off.

'Walk,' he said to Missy, and she did as gracefully as a duchess with Jane up, her back straighter now, moving slowly with no attempt at a trot, going tentatively around the field. They did a complete circle of the paddock before coming to a stop again by the stables – and when Simon drew up alongside her he reined in his horse and stepped down.

He held out his arms and she slid into them. He kept them around her for the briefest moment. How tiny she was, how fragile – but she didn't meet his eyes until he let her go when her lashes fluttered and she opened wide dark eyes to his. He saw that they were wet with tears.

'Thank you,' she breathed. 'Thank you.'

'You'll be all right now,' he said as Susannah came towards them.

'Well, well, well. Did you work a miracle?'

'Yes, Jane told me she hadn't ridden since...'

'And now she has.' Was there the merest hint of coolness in Susannah's voice?

Jane stood quite still as her cousin mounted Missy and waited for Simon. Once he was alongside her, she tapped the mare sharply and raced away towards the meadow, Simon behind her. He had never felt more miserable in his life.

Constance arrived home around five in the afternoon. She changed, brushed and hung up her suit on its hanger, putting the blouse and her tights aside for washing. Her help, Mrs Naughton, was excellent at that. Then she changed her shoes and put on a housecoat. She sorted her notes and filed them in one of the cabinets in the study. She could always put her hand on anything she wanted so thorough was she in her record-keeping.

She had bathed by five-thirty and made

herself a cup of tea to drink before getting dressed again when she was surprised by the front doorbell. Glancing through the bedroom window, she saw her son Dennis's car parked on the drive and heard his key turn in the lock. Constance frowned. What on earth could he be doing here at this hour?

'Mother?'

'I'm upstairs, dear, be down in a minute.' His arrival reminded her that she really must write to Eloise, her daughter. The trouble was Constance had forgotten just where she was – Australia or was it Zimbabwe?

'Coming, dear.' And she sailed down the staircase, one white beringed hand resting regally on the banister. Dennis came forward to greet her, kissing her lightly.

'And to what do I owe the pleasure at this time of day?' his mother enquired.

'I was on my way home and thought I'd call in – I won't stay long. Is Dad home yet?'

'No, not yet. We're off to a council meeting this evening.'

'Oh, well, I won't keep you.'

'Oh, we don't go out until seven-thirty. Can I get you something – tea, coffee, a glass of wine?'

'No, thanks, Mother. I only called in, as I say.'

He sat himself down on the largest chair. Dennis was a rather big young man with a shock of curly hair. He looked like his father had once except that he didn't have his father's strong chin. Or character.

'By the way, how was the engagement party – you did go, didn't you?' Constance asked.

'Oh, yes, it was quite a bash, lots of very interesting people there. The cousin from America, for instance.'

'Yes, I'd heard she was there. Rather a tragic time for her, I imagine?'

'Yes. Pretty girl, though, typically American.'

I hope, Constance thought wearily, he hasn't been up to any of his tricks.

'Fact is, Mother, I thought I'd let you know that Saskia and I are split – er – separating.'

She turned flashing dark eyes on him. 'Separating! But you've only been together six months.'

'I know.' And Dennis looked quite sorry for himself. 'It's a pity but there it is. It's a no-win situation, I'm afraid.' And he looked once again like the little boy he used to be.

A fine kettle of fish, she told herself. He'd already had several 'serious' relationships, none of them fated to be permanent.

'Well,' she sighed heavily, 'you know best. You wouldn't think of counselling?'

'Good Lord, no!' He seemed quite shocked by the suggestion.

'Well, don't tell me about it – I'd rather not know. I'm very sorry – I don't know what else to say. I don't understand young people today. I was hoping you'd settle down this time and it would actually last. I liked Saskia.'

'So did I, at first. But ... well...'

He stood up, relieved he had got the unpleasant few minutes over.

'Well, I'd better go. Give Dad my love.'

Closing the door on him, Constance couldn't help wondering what was the matter with young people today. Goodness knows she came across enough of them in her counselling capacity.

Dennis had had everything it was possible for a boy to have: a splendid education, prep school at eight followed by public school. He hadn't been to university though they would have supported him gladly. Wasn't the type, he'd said.

She sighed again at the thought of her wastrel son. Well, no one could blame her or Geoffrey. They had done absolutely everything for him. His first car at eighteen, a small boat – and the flat in town they had bought for him. The trouble was the girls had always flocked around him.

She idled through the stack of cards on the desk. Ah, here was the last card from Eloise. Constance turned it over. Oh, New Zealand. Well, she'd known it was somewhere like that.

Roll on Friday, her long-anticipated evening off.

Barbara couldn't wait to tell Viv about her experiences at the charity shop. That evening she telephoned her.

'Oh, come round,' Viv told her. 'I'm feeling very low at the moment.'

And I'm not surprised, Barbara thought. With that nice husband all those miles away. It was bad enough when you had to be alone, let alone choosing to be.

She found Viv finishing the ironing.

'One thing about the summer,' she said, 'there's not so much washing and ironing to do. It's the winter months I hate – all those woollies, thick shirts and trousers. I'll put the coffee on.'

Somehow, Barbara thought, you could sense there wasn't a man around the house.

George's absence was almost tangible. She could see little Ben in the back garden, playing with his toys on this summer evening, but there was no evidence of George's shirts on the airer. Didn't Viv miss him?

Barbara told her about the shop and soon Viv was laughing as she made the coffee and got out a cake.

'I've often wondered what it would be like to work in one of those shops. I don't think I could – ugh! All those awful old castoffs.'

'It's quite hard, you don't get a minute to yourself, but great fun of course. I've only done one day so far, but I'm quite looking forward to Thursday.'

Viv looked up suddenly. 'I'm glad we got to know each other,' she said. 'It's nice to have a friend to talk to. I miss my old friends.'

Barbara looked pleased.

'Me too,' she said. 'My life has totally changed since I left the bookshop.'

'Mine, too,' Viv said, 'since George left.'

'Ah, but you have a solution to that.'

'What, give in and go to the States?' Viv looked astonished. 'Never! He knows, Barbara, that if he's determined to stay over there, our marriage is over – finished.'

'Oh, Viv, you can't mean it!'

'I couldn't be more serious. I shall take

Ben over there for two weeks before he goes back to school and if George has really made up his mind, then that's that.' She spoke with such conviction Barbara knew she meant it.

Simon drove over to Kirby Lodge on Thursday, ten days before the wedding, his mind in a turmoil such as he had never experienced before.

He had to get this thing sorted out, though God alone knew how. He had never in his life felt like this about a woman, and it wasn't as if he really knew her. He had met Jane twice and in that short space of time she had set his heart on fire.

He knew he was asking for trouble. What did he hope to achieve? This girl had recently lost a dearly loved fiancé, she was vulnerable, how would this visit of his make any sense? What would it solve?

Simon loved Susannah with all his heart, he knew he did. It had been all he'd ever wanted: to marry her, have children and grow old together. What then was this about? That the sight of those great dark eyes filled him with compassion – was that all it was? Pity for Jane? Sympathy? But he knew it was more than that. He wanted to

whisk her away from everyone and everything and take care of her. Susannah had
never inspired protective feelings like this.
She was strong, efficient, capable – theirs
was a marriage approved of by everyone.
Perhaps that was the trouble. Susannah was
like a friend he had known forever, she'd
certainly never inspired passion within him,
she was easy to be with, they were good
friends.

But the other girl, Jane, the moment he'd
held her it had seemed as if he was on fire.
It was like an electric shock, the feel of her,
holding her. He had never wanted to let go.

But what was he achieving by driving over
to Birch Common in this state ten days
before the wedding? He must be mad. He
only knew he had to see her again and
believed she felt the same, had gone through
the same emotions that had flooded him.
And if she had, what was the answer?

Well, it was simple. He couldn't marry
Susannah feeling as he did about Jane,
though the ramifications were too awful to
contemplate.

But could he go through with marriage,
knowing he had fallen blindly in love with
someone else?

He had had other girl friends but so far as

marriage went it had always been Susannah. Now her cousin had set his pulses racing, his heart pounding, and it was something he was sure that she felt too.

He imagined himself and Susannah, bride and groom, standing at the altar. She made a beautiful bride, as he'd always known she would, and he stood by her side, living a lie. No, it wasn't fair to her. Better to finish it now than go through a ceremony just for the sake of pleasing everyone else.

It would, of course, break Susannah's heart, and at this point he slowed down the car and pulled in to a lay-by.

Christ! What was he about to do? What did he hope to achieve? Better turn back now before any more damage was done. But he felt sick inside. He couldn't go through with the wedding feeling like this. Perhaps if he could see Jane again, just once, it might put his mind at rest. So far he had spent two sleepless nights thinking about her.

He pulled out into the traffic and went on his way to Birch Common.

It was ten-thirty when his car pulled up outside the house, and he noticed straight away that there were no others parked there. Perhaps just as well, he thought. Mounting the steps, he rang the bell.

The housekeeper answered and smiled at him in greeting.

'Oh, Mr Rawnsley, come in although I'm afraid there's no one here. Mrs Whittaker and Susannah have gone to Texbury and Mr Whittaker is in the City today.'

But Jane, where was she? he wanted to ask.

'I see. Well, it's not important, Mrs Adams. Have you any idea when they'll be back?'

Now he was here he couldn't think what to say because he only wanted to see Jane. More than anything, he wanted to see her.

'They shouldn't be long. Certainly back before twelve, I should think.'

'I'll hang about then. Go over to the stables,' he said. 'Tell them where I am when they get back.'

He would ride, he thought. Try and dissipate this unsettling passion. He would strike out for the meadow then on to the fields.

Jane was in the stables as he'd half known she would be, just dismounting, patting the mare's head. Looking up, she saw him approach. Beneath that magnolia skin was a deep telltale flush.

She spoke first, softly – almost in a whisper.

'Simon.'

He stood looking at her.

'They're not here, they've...'

'I know. Mrs Adams told me.'

She had composed herself now, and smiled at him.

'Have you come to ride? I've just been. It's glorious out there.'

He walked over to her, and put both his hands on her shoulders.

'Jane, I have to talk to you.'

She wriggled away from beneath his grasp.

'Simon, please.'

He bent forward and kissed her lightly, feeling the answering pressure from her soft lips, the current that flowed between them, and exulted, knowing he was right, surprised to find he was trembling.

'Simon, we can't–' And then, to shatter the dream, the sound of a car and Jane began to run across the yard, taking off her gloves as she did so.

'Oh!' she cried. 'There you are. I've just been for a glorious ride – it was wonderful!'

Slowly Simon followed her, his expression inscrutable as he kissed first Susannah and then Anne.

'Sorry I missed you,' Susannah said. 'Did you get a ride in, Simon?'

'No, I only just got here.'

'Oh, well, it's almost time for a lunchtime drink,' she said, putting her arm through his and going up the steps.

'I must go and change,' Jane said.

'I'm glad you're riding again,' Anne told her. 'It's done you the world of good.'

'Actually,' Simon said, 'I won't stay. I've got to get back. Pa's waiting for me, but there was some query about the timing for the reception..'

'Oh, well, you'd better have that drink then. This could take all day,' Susannah laughed.

On the way home Simon berated himself: 'You haven't got the courage of a flea.' And now, even more than when he'd set out, he felt he could not possibly go through with the wedding, whatever the outcome.

Tonight he would tell Gil – he was Simon's closest friend and as his best man at the wedding, it seemed the logical thing to do.

Later on they sat together in his father's library over a whisky and soda. It wasn't Simon's usual drink but he felt the need for it tonight.

Gil wondered what Simon had to say.

Something about the wedding probably. He certainly seemed agitated. Gil sat back, looking politely attentive, as he had learned to do whenever the subject of Susannah came up. A tall, dark, good-looking man, he had been at college with Simon and knew him as well as he knew his own family.

When Simon blurted out his story, Gil said nothing for quite some time.

'What do you want me to say?' he said finally.

'I can't go through with the wedding, Gil, you do see that, don't you?'

'No, I'm not with you, I'm afraid, Simon.' Inwardly he was seething. 'Attractive though this young woman is that's no excuse for calling off a wedding. What's got into you, Si?'

'I just can't go through with it. It wouldn't be fair to Susannah, feeling as I do about someone else.'

'Balls! You're just suffering from pre-wedding nerves,' Gil insisted.

'No, I know how I feel.'

'It's basically called sex. Fatal attraction and all that.'

'Don't be so bloody stupid,' Simon said, ruffled now. 'I'd just like to spend the rest of my life with her.'

'But you don't even know her,' Gil said, his eyes like flint.

'It doesn't matter, she's the one.'

'Well,' Gil downed his drink, 'I don't know whether you came to me for sympathy but I can't take any more of this talk. I'll see you at the ceremony on Saturday unless there's anything else you need to confide in me before then.' And he walked out, slamming the door behind him.

Simon had never seen his friend so rattled. Fat chance of any sympathy there.

He went to bed and dreamed of Jane, with her dark brown eyes and touch like fire.

The next morning, Jane was down before her cousin. Anne Whittaker was an early riser and Jane knew she would find her in the kitchen preparing breakfast.

'Oh, good morning, Jane. Did you sleep well?'

Anne glanced across at her niece and saw the dark shadows under her eyes.

'Aunt Anne, I don't know how to say this but would you mind very much if I went home?'

Anne sat down abruptly.

'Went home? Whatever for, child? I thought you were enjoying yourself?'

'Yes, I am, and you've been very kind. But, well, I just can't go through with the wedding bit. I shall be so unhappy thinking about ... well, what might have been.'

'Oh, my dear.' And Anne came over and put an arm around her. 'I do understand. But by Saturday...'

Jane shook her head vehemently. 'No, I mean it. I've really loved seeing you and Uncle Eric and Susannah again – and getting back on a horse.' She smiled ruefully. 'But it's more than I can do to stay for the wedding.'

'Well, there are a few days yet.'

'No, I've made up my mind,' Jane said firmly.

'Well, dear, you know best. I'll get Uncle Eric to book you a flight.'

Jane closed the kitchen door softly, and stood with her back against it, her eyes filled with tears.

As the organ pealed out in the little church, and Simon stood waiting with Gil at his side, Susannah entered followed by her two bridesmaids, a vision of loveliness. There were 'oohs' and 'aahs' as she went down the aisle on the arm of her father, head held high, eyes bluer than ever.

Simon turned his head to look down at her, and at his side Gil made sure he had the wedding ring in his pocket.

He watched her, beautiful in her bridal gown, the girl he had been in love with ever since he'd first met her. He would have given his eye teeth to be in Simon's place.

Chapter Six

In the luxury hotel bedroom, Susannah lay awake. The clock on the bedside table showed it was five-thirty in the morning and, turning her head, she saw Simon's fair hair on the pillow beside her. She took a deep breath and ran one hand over her body – naked as the day she was born – and with her foot reached down for the slip of a nightie, sheer French satin encrusted with lace, bringing it up towards her by her toes. She waited for the sensation of complete and utter fulfilment she had felt at other times like this. Of course, she had slept with Simon before – not all that many times, but on every previous occasion there had been the sheer exhaustion of successful love making, the delicious satisfaction of two people deeply in love coming together, the blissful state of bodies sated, the luxurious sense of inertia.

But here she was now, awake at five-thirty – wide awake.

Of course she was overtired, it was all the

excitement. What a wedding it had been! She knew she had looked as wonderful as every bride should on her wedding day, and now she was Mrs Simon Rawnsley, one day to be Lady Rawnsley. But that was not why she had married him. She put out her hand and touched his face tentatively. She loved him so much. Perhaps, she thought, it was being given permission – actually being married – that dispelled the feeling you were being wicked when you made unmarried love. The element of daring was no longer there. At all events, it had not been as exciting as on previous occasions when they had stolen away for a few hours to be by themselves.

Neither she nor Simon had had boy or girl friends since the age of sixteen when they had first teamed up. Well, she didn't *think* Simon had – she was sure she would have known if so.

They were like a couple of kids, she thought, set free from parental strings. She couldn't imagine being married to anyone else. She had never seen him look at any other girl – well, just that once when Jane had turned up. Still, you couldn't count her, pretty though she was. She wasn't Simon's type, and he had felt desperately sorry for her, you could see. Strange how she had gone back home so suddenly. Well, a good thing really, she hadn't been happy, and it would have been awful having her around on the day itself, grieving for what might have been.

Forgetting her cousin in an instant as Simon opened his eyes wide and looked at her, Susannah leaned over and kissed him. 'Happy honeymoon, darling.' And throwing her nightie to the floor, she eased herself into his arms and lowered her mouth to his.

'Darling, darling, Simon...'

Later, she stood at the window while he was in the bathroom, looking out at the palm trees, the white surf, the golden sands, the great heart-shaped swimming pool – it was all exactly as she had imagined it.

Simon came up behind her, putting his arms round her.

'Happy?' he asked, kissing her hair.

She turned round to face him.

'Blissfully,' she said, eyes closed. 'I love you, Simon.'

'And I love you, too,' he said softly, looking out beyond her to the blue sea and golden sands, but not seeing them.

He did love her. He loved her dearly – she was closer to him than anyone in the world.

Why then was there a picture in front of him always of a wisp of a girl with dark curly hair and serious brown eyes, a girl who had the power to capture his heart however hard he tried to escape? Susannah reached up to kiss him.

'Let's have breakfast,' she said. 'I'm starving.'

Barbara was into her second week at the charity shop and enjoying it. The time passed so quickly when she was there, they were all so busy doing something or other, it simply flew by.

It was like a giant cement mixer. The stuff came in at one end of the shop and went straight out the other. Gladys was an excellent organiser, never in any doubt when a decision had to be made.

When bags of old shoes long past repair, or shirts and pyjamas that had seen better days, arrived, her decision was swift and to the point.

'Bin them,' she said, no questions asked. Some things were washed – those that were worth it – in her own home, and there was an ironing machine in the shop and a steamer that made short work of wrinkled garments. Pricing was done by volunteers, the garments then hung on hangers according to colour and size. Barbara liked it when the young housewives came in, usually pushing a pram, going through the shirts until they found what they wanted.

Some of them were excellent quality and had originally been expensive, and Barbara always enjoyed it when a young woman found something that was a real bargain.

'That's very nice,' she would say. 'A very good quality shirt.'

'No need to tell them that, they know when they're getting a bargain,' Gladys said, aware of how much work had gone into their sorting.

Old men came in for clothes, overcoats and suits, children for toys, young girls hoping to find something belonging to a past era. Large ladies looking for large sizes. Young men looking for CDs and 78s alike.

One day a tiny timid-looking Asian girl came in, looking no more than sixteen.

'Have you a wedding dress?' she asked.

Barbara wanted to ask, 'A proper wedding dress?' Imagining that the girl would surely wear a sari to her own wedding. But she couldn't be nosy. 'I'm not sure – I haven't seen one. I'll just check with the manageress,' she told the girl.

Gladys came out for a moment and looked hard at the girl.

'What size are you?' she asked severely. No sentiment there, thought Barbara.

'I don't know...'

'Is it for you?'

The girl nodded.

'Just a moment.'

Gladys disappeared and presently came back with a large cardboard box which she opened to reveal a magnificent silk wedding gown elaborately adorned with pearls. She took it from the box carefully and held it out. Inside was a prestigious designer label. Barbara gasped.

'Too big for you,' Gladys said, frowning at the girl. 'You'd swim in it.'

'I can try?' she asked.

'You can try with pleasure,' Gladys said, 'but I tell you, you'll swim in it.'

She stood by frowning while Barbara couldn't wait to see the girl emerge from the cubicle.

Well, of course, the gown was magnificent on – a true model gown – but Gladys was quite right, it was miles too big for the girl.

'I will alter,' she said.

'You'd have to remake it,' Gladys objected.

'How much is it?'

Gladys thought hard. 'Thirty-five pounds,' she said at length, and Barbara gave an inward gasp. Obviously worn only once, it must have cost hundreds if not thousands of pounds. Just imagine trying to alter those extra-fine, almost invisible seams...

'Is there a veil?' the girl asked.

She looked so incongruous standing there. The dress was miles too long, spread out over the floor and falling off her shoulders as well as being twice the size she needed. You could have cut it in half, Barbara thought.

'I'll see,' Gladys said and disappeared again.

This time she brought forth another large flat box in which was a splendid veil, full-length, and a tiara of pearls obviously matching the gown.

The girl emerged from the cubicle looking like a five year old dressed up in her mother's clothes.

'Fifty quid the lot,' Gladys said. She seemed to know the girl was going to have it.

'I take it,' she said, and clad in her finery disappeared back into the cubicle.

Barbara was mesmerised, but Gladys was obviously used to such moments.

'You want cash,' she said, 'and pack it carefully.'

The girl re-appeared, dragging the wedding gown, and looked in her purse, counting out four ten-pound notes and two fives.

Gladys appeared again and examined the notes closely, holding them up to the light, marking with her special scratcher.

'Ring up fifty pounds,' she said, 'under DRESSES.' And that was that.

Never a dull moment, Barbara thought, and looked up as four tall schoolboys came in.

'Ah, there you are,' Gladys said. 'Get in there and start marking, you know your way. You'll find the trousers all ready and the shirts on the rail.'

'From the local comprehensive,' she explained. 'They all have to do their bit.'

When Barbara went into the kitchen later they were sitting on the floor working diligently, stapling priced tickets on to the garments.

'Nearly one,' a boy said. 'I'm starving.'

'Yeah, we're nearly finished. We'll be out of your way in a sec, Mrs.'

Who could complain about the youth of today? wondered Barbara.

Just as she withdrew her handbag from the

drawer a young girl came in, wearing white shorts, very high heels and a baseball cap – and the Versace jacket. I'd forgotten about that, Barbara thought.

She couldn't wait to see Viv and tell her all about it.

Ben was staying with Viv's mother overnight when Barbara called round for a drink. They sat in the garden, eating olives and nuts, while Viv listened fascinated to stories of the charity shop and the wedding dress.

'I have to say it was the most beautiful wedding dress I have ever seen,' Barbara said, thinking of her own which had been lovely, of course, but nothing like as exotic or ornate as the Indian girl's purchase.

'I can't begin to think how she will alter it – it was enormous on her and all that decoration.'

'Well, Indian clothes can be very ornate too. Think of all the embroidery and the beading you see.'

'Yes, that's true,' Barbara agreed, and thinking of weddings suddenly felt newly miserable at the thought of being alone.

Noticing her expression, Viv topped up her wine and held out the olives.

'Well, only two more weeks and Ben and I

are off to the States,' she said, knowing that would shake Barbara out of her apathy.

'So soon!' she cried. 'I'd forgotten you were going at the end of August.'

'It's to fit in with Ben's school term. He'll already miss four days. Still, can't be helped. I did explain we were going to see his father in America and that was the only convenient time.'

'Are you getting excited?' Barbara asked.

'Why?'

'To be seeing George again.'

'Oh, yes, that. But not the rest of it. I hate flying and the States has never appealed to me.'

There was no point badgering her about it, Barbara decided. Not even the thought of seeing her husband again could rouse Viv's enthusiasm.

'You must let me know if there is anything I can do,' she said. 'While you're away, I mean.'

'My mother will come and feed Oscar.'

'Ask her to let me know if she needs anything,' Barbara said. 'Well, I suppose I'd better go.'

'When's your trip to India?'

'Beginning of February. It can't come round soon enough.'

Rather you than me, Viv thought.

As the time drew nearer for Viv and Ben to depart Barbara knew she was going to miss them more than she had thought – and to think this time last year she hadn't even known them.

'How are you getting to Heathrow?' she asked.

'Taxi,' Viv said. 'No point in taking the car to rack up parking charges.'

'I'll take you,' Barbara offered.

'Oh, no, it's sweet of you, but...'

'I'd like to,' she said. 'Give me something to do.'

'Oh, well, in that case,' Viv laughed.

Once they had disappeared and made for the check-in desk Barbara made her way out of the airport and back to the parking lot, stopping once on her way home for coffee. Afterwards, as the planes soared above her one after another, she wondered which one they were on. Little Ben had been so excited.

She thought she might do a couple of extra mornings at the charity shop while they were away. Gladys might even find another wedding dress – and she remembered the little Indian girl.

Oh, roll on February.

Susannah and Simon had settled into the Dower House on the Rawnsley estate. It had been decided that since Lord and Lady Rawnsley were still young, only in their late-fifties, they would stay in the big house while the Dower House would be renovated for the newly weds.

The Rawnsleys had decided that on the birth of their first grandchild they would move out of Fulford Manor and either move away to their home in Scotland or take over the Dower House.

It was a dear little place, smaller than anything Susannah had been used to but now decorated to her choice, with an extra bathroom for guests, and a conservatory extension on to the drawing room which served as a dining room, the whole place being set in a lovely garden. Susannah thought it like a doll's house but very much her own home. The kitchen was a showpiece of designer units and not far from the stable yard where she and Simon kept their horses, for the Rawnsleys no longer rode to hounds.

Time hung heavily. She shared the house-keeper at Fulford Manor so there was little for her to do. Susannah took to driving home to Birch Common when Simon was at the office in Reading which he shared with Gilroy Maclean. As architects they had a small practice which they hoped to expand as their reputation grew. They had met at architectural college and liked each other immediately. Undoubtedly gifted as he was, Simon's family background stood him in good stead while Gil had had to work for his success every inch of the way.

Susannah enjoyed the days that the house was open to the public. It gave her something to do, assisting her mother-in-law with the extra work these visitors' days entailed.

She had been toying with the idea of starting riding classes again for disabled children. It was something she had enjoyed doing once a week back at Kirby Lodge, and there was no reason why she should not do it here.

She and Simon rode first thing, weather permitting, and often walked round the estate after dinner in the summer months. She was immensely proud of the future in store for her, and couldn't wait for her first baby to arrive. She secretly thought she was much more proud of the Rawnsley heritage than Simon was, and realised that was because he was used to it, born into it, and took it all for granted.

Married life had not proved to be quite so exciting as she had imagined. Life at Kirby Lodge had never been dull – her mother had seen to that. There had been the riding classes and helping out at the Blind School, something her father had encouraged her to do since he was on the board of governors. But at Fulford Lady Rawnsley was totally taken up with the house and her money-raising efforts, and Lord Rawnsley, though a dear, seemed to belong to another world.

There was a touch of autumn in the air when Susannah drove over to Kirby Lodge. As she approached Birch Common from Texbury she smiled to see her home – and had to admit to herself it was still home as Fulford Manor had never been. Not yet, at any rate.

Her mother came out to meet her, running down the steps like a two year old, her figure slight in narrow cream slacks and a pale blue polo neck to match her eyes.

'Oh, darling, it's lovely to see you.' They kissed warmly. 'Just in time for lunch but we'll have a drink first – we're celebrating.'

Susannah laughed. 'Celebrating what?'

'Any excuse.' Anne squeezed her arm as they went into the house. 'Your father and I have decided to take a little trip.'

'Oh, Mummy, that's great! When? Where?'

'We're going to the States, to New York, to see your Aunt Felicity. Our visit's long overdue.'

'Why, that's wonderful!' Susannah was genuinely pleased although she knew she would miss them. 'How long will you be gone?'

'About a month, we thought. A couple of weeks with Felicity then on to California to see our old friends the Goodwins. Do you remember them?'

'Of course I do. They used to bring me the most wonderful presents.'

'They certainly did. Ah, here's your father.'

The sight of his daughter was enough to bring a smile to Eric's usual stern face.

'Susannah, how lovely to see you.' And she realised how much he missed her. She linked her arm through his.

'Now tell me about this jaunt of yours,' she said as they walked into the drawing room.

She would miss them, she thought. A whole month – what would she do with herself? She knew everyone thought she was lucky, marrying a handsome young man like Simon who adored her, going from one lovely home to another – but was it always like this when you first married? She had loved her life and her home and her parents – the break had been quite difficult for her. She supposed that was why people had honeymoons, to mark the change from one lifestyle to another.

Still, she must think about the baby yet to come. Who knew? This month perhaps.

'What news of Jane?' she asked.

'Not a lot,' Anne said, sipping her dry martini. 'Apparently, she spends a lot of time on her own. I think Felicity is quite worried about her – says she doesn't eat, spends most of her time in Virginia. I expect we shall hear more about it when we get there.'

'Well, I don't suppose she's got over the shock yet,' Susannah said. 'After all, it's still early days. Only a few months since...'

'True.' Anne sighed then took a deep breath.

'How's Simon?' she asked.

Ben was beside himself with excitement on the long plane trip. His parents seemed pleased to see each other again. His father met them at the airport and took them back to his rooms at the university in the biggest car Ben had ever seen. He looked around him on the drive, at the palm trees and sometimes beaches. The sun was hot and shone all the time and never seemed to go in like it did at home.

The college campus, as his father called it, was enormous. There was a huge white building with small ones around it. The place was quiet, his father said, because term didn't officially start until next week.

George put his arm round Viv's shoulders. 'God, I've missed you,' he said.

'I've missed you too,' she replied, and knew that in all truth she had. When he kissed her later it was just like old times. If only, she thought, he would come home and stop all this messing about.

George had two rooms plus a little kitchen and bathroom. The bedroom had two single beds, and Ben slept on the sofa bed in the living room.

Later, when he was tucked up asleep, Viv and George curled up together on one of the beds and made love much as they had done when they'd first married.

'We belong together,' he said. 'We're no good apart.'

Viv sat up, her eyes shining. 'Oh, darling, does that mean you'll come home?'

George lay with his arms behind his head,

staring at her.

'I was hoping,' he said miserably, 'you might have changed your mind.'

Viv went back to her own bed without another word.

The next night they tumbled on to one single bed again. 'I'm sorry,' George said afterwards.

'So am I,' Viv said – but she still ended up on the other single bed.

She lay in the dark, eyes wide open. I do love him, she decided. I do. And I want Ben to have his father with him. But I can't – I just can't – come and live here. I like where I am. I like my job, I like my house, my mother is there. Why should I give in? I want George to come home.

He slept almost at once. If Viv thought she was going to get round him...

Sometimes Ben could hear his parents talking, sometimes arguing, and he could tell that it was much the same as it had been at home. It was pretty obvious his mother was not happy on this holiday. Neither was his father, come to that. In the daytime they spent lots of time swimming, and he saw the dolphins, and his father took him to the base-ball pitch, and then they went to the Kennedy Space Centre. That was the highlight of his trip and Ben talked of little else.

Although they did all these things, Ben still felt there was something missing. It was almost as if his father liked America better than he liked being home with Ben and his mother.

'Can't we come and live in America with Daddy?' he asked. 'Gran could come too.' It seemed a reasonable enough request.

'No, darling, we belong at home.'

'So does Dad,' Ben said, and his mother held him tightly.

When they left for the airport, Ben sat behind his parents in the car. He could hear them although they spoke in low tones.

'Things haven't changed then?' his mother said.

'I was hoping you might feel differently,' George said.

'You mean, come round to your way of thinking? No, I'm afraid it's too big a decision.'

'I'll be home at Christmas.'

'And when you come, I hope it will be for keeps. Otherwise...' Viv left the outcome unsaid.

'You mean, we're finished?'

'As simple as that,' she said.

The car pulled in at the terminal, and

George kissed Ben and Viv goodbye.

'See you at Christmas,' he said. He remembered her previous threat that if he didn't come home after the holiday it was all over between them. He waited for her to tell him she wanted an official separation.

'We'll be at the airport to meet you,' Viv said, looking straight into his eyes.

His father picked Ben up and held him high in the air before putting him down.

''Bye now, Sunny Jim,' he said. 'Take care of your mother.'

When Ben looked up at her, he saw that her eyes were full of tears.

Chapter Seven

'So how did you get on?' Barbara asked as she and Viv sat in her garden drinking tea. 'How was George?'

'Oh, he was fine,' Viv said wearily. 'But you know, Barbara, the more I see of life over there, the more I dislike it. I just couldn't settle there. It's a lifestyle that's completely alien to me.'

Barbara was worried, for Ben as well as for Viv.

She sighed. 'It seems such a pity, though. You love George. I should have thought anywhere he was, you would be happy.'

'Then I obviously don't love him enough,' Viv said. 'To be honest – and I have thought about it, seriously – I would rather be here on my own with Ben than in the States with George. If, somehow or other, he had Ben over there with him, then I could be pushed, but since that's not likely, it looks like I'm here to stay. Oh, it's all right for the odd holiday, but other than that – no, I couldn't.'

'I wonder ... I mean, don't you miss him as

a husband? A friend? A man about the house?'

'Well...'

'Of course, you have Ben.'

'But that's not what you meant, is it?'

'No.'

'You mean, for sex?'

Barbara flushed. 'No, not altogether. I mean, I'd give anything to have William back. I hate living on my own.'

Viv thought about it. 'As you say, I have Ben – but I don't think I feel like that. I quite like my own company, don't feel a man is absolutely necessary in my life.'

'That's interesting,' Barbara mused. 'I think perhaps some people are meant not to be alone, and I'm one of them.'

'But you have things to do now. Look how busy you've become in the last few months.'

'Yes, I know, my life has really picked up. But I need someone to share it with, don't you understand that?'

'No,' Viv said honestly. 'I'd rather be alone than share it with someone I didn't care about or disliked.'

'But you love George.'

'Then, obviously, not enough,' Viv said. 'Besides, like him, you're overlooking my job. I'm doing very well and a promotion has definitely been promised now. What would I do about that? I don't want to give it up.'

'Couldn't you get a similar job over there?'

'And start all over again? I'm not George with his special qualifications, but my job is every bit as important to me as George's is to him.'

Stalemate, thought Barbara.

'I did wonder recently whether I might try for a job in publishing, too. I used to be Chief Librarian in the public library, you know.'

'Did you?' Viv looked impressed. 'Well, I don't see why not. It's the same field, isn't it? Books.' And they laughed together. 'Do you want me to sound it out for you?'

'Oh, if you would. Except I have no qualifications in the publishing world – what would I do?'

'Let's think about it,' Viv said, and stirred her tea. 'He's coming home for Christmas,' she said at length.

Barbara brightened.

'Who? George? Oh, I am glad,' she said.

Around six-thirty, Susannah pulled up outside her parents' home and saw Dennis Pargetter-Wilson walking across the common towards his mother's house.

'Hi there, Dennis,' she said, getting out of the car. 'What are you doing down here?'

'Same as you, I expect. I've just walked up from the station – car's in dock.'

'Oh, I'm sorry. I'm going to dinner with my parents.'

'And I'm just calling in to see Ma. Care for a drink first?'

Susannah glanced across the common towards The Bear.

'Why not?' she asked, and fell into step beside him.

Once in the bar he ordered and came back to their table in the corner.

'So how's married life?'

Knowing he could have only one thing in mind with that question, Susannah smiled.

'Perfect,' she said.

'Where is Mr Wonderful this evening?'

'In Scotland,' Susannah said. 'He and Gil have gone up to Edinburgh – they have a possible commission up there. They've done their presentation, submitted their estimate, and it seems they might have a real chance of getting the work.'

'Leaving the poor little bride on her own?' sympathised Dennis with one of his soulful looks.

He had a habit of looking straight into your eyes when he made remarks like that, and Susannah squirmed inwardly. In truth, she had thought Gil could deal with this on his own.

'And what about you?' she countered. 'Your girl friend? Sorry, I've forgotten...'

'Now, now, Susannah,' he said. 'You must remember Joanna? She was at the wedding.'

'Oh, yes, of course, Joanna.' Although in truth she didn't recall any of the guests. It had been such a whirlwind of a day, and Dennis had had so many girl friends it was difficult to keep count. She was sure the latest was called Saskia – must be out of date on his love life.

'You're looking absolutely fantastic,' he said, openly appraising her, although he secretly thought she looked a tad weary about the eyes. There was a little frown line that seemed to be new. Dennis was knowledgeable about women; had had a lot of experience.

She was obviously pleased with his compliment.

'Thank you,' she said. He looked quite dishy himself, which was why he could always find a girl. She had found him attractive at one time until her parents had laid down the law.

She had heard her father say one day, 'This must be nipped in the bud before it goes any farther, Anne. Dennis is a most unsuitable young man.'

Susannah had been upset at the time, not understanding, because Dennis was fun and good for a laugh. But as time went by, she knew how she would feel if her own daughter, as yet unborn, had Dennis Pargetter-Wilson in mind as a possible husband. Still, he knew how to give a girl a good time. She glanced at him surreptitiously, wondering what it was about him that tipped people off he was a bit of a waster. Tall, well-built, nice eyes. Perhaps the chin was a little weak, but then he had been hopelessly spoiled as a child.

He had been given everything he could possibly want except perhaps attention. His mother had been so steeped in good works for others that she'd scarcely had time for him. A succession of nannies, chauffeured to school each day until he went to boarding school, the first sports car any of their crowd had had – oh, yes, he had been spoiled. And was certainly not to be compared with Simon who was a different breed altogether.

'I believe your parents have been visiting

America,' he said presently. 'How is that little cousin of yours? Jane, wasn't it?'

Susannah nodded.

'Pretty little thing, she wowed us all – quite bowled us over. Er, how is she? Lost her fiancé, that right?'

'Yes, it was tragic.'

'Pity she didn't stay for the wedding but under the circs, I suppose...'

'Oh, yes,' Susannah said, finishing her drink. 'Look, I must go. I said I'd be there around seven.'

She didn't tell him she was anxious to hear all about their trip. They had only been home two days, but somehow the question of Jane nagged at Susannah. How had she been on her return home?

'Sure,' he said. 'It was nice seeing you. I don't often come down from town these days.'

'I'm sure your mother is always pleased when you do.'

With this banal remark, Susannah walked through the door he'd opened for her and they strolled back across the common together.

'Give my love to your mother,' she said as Dennis kissed her lightly on the cheek. Seeing that lovely face so close to his, he couldn't resist putting his arms around her, too.

She pushed him away. 'Oh, grow up, Dennis!' she said irritably. 'Get a life! Isn't it time you were married and settled down?' Knowing that part of her reaction stemmed from her own far from perfect marriage, she walked away up to Kirby Lodge.

'My regards to your parents,' Dennis called after her. He was not easily fazed. He walked on to The Cedars, letting himself in with his key.

'Ma?' he called. 'It's me – Dennis.'

A voice drifted down from upstairs.

'Oh! I wondered who it was. You gave me a fright. Where's your car?'

'It's in dock, I took the train.'

His mother came down the stairs, a substantial vision in black, obviously dressed for going out later.

They kissed and Constance walked into the kitchen. He followed her.

'Is everything all right?' she asked. He usually only appeared when he wanted something, though she hated to admit this to herself.

'No, everything's fine although I did want a word with Dad. Is he going to be in?'

'Yes.' She glanced at her watch. 'In about

141

half an hour. Help yourself to a drink, I'll be with you later.'

She disappeared as he helped himself to whisky in the dining room and wandered around, glass in hand, in search of her.

'I've just seen Susannah – Susannah Whittaker that was.'

Constance felt a moment's trepidation as she always did when a girl's name was mentioned.

'She's down to have dinner with her parents – Simon's away. We had a drink at The Bear.'

At this his mother's heart sank. He wasn't up to his old tricks, was he?

'That's nice,' Constance said calmly. 'How's Joanna by the way?'

'She's in Paris on some business trip or other. Back tomorrow.'

Thank God for that. Constance quite liked Joanna – thought her a calming influence, if such a thing were possible with Dennis.

'Look, you get going if you have to,' he said. 'I'll wait here for Dad.'

She turned apprehensive eyes to him.

'You're not ... there's no problem, is there? Financial or otherwise?'

'Good Lord, no,' he laughed as if the idea

was inconceivable. 'Where are you bound for?'

'Council meeting,' she said.

'Dad not going?'

'Not this evening,' she said, pulling on her gloves.

'By the way,' he said. 'Joanna and I have booked a holiday for the New Year. Well, February, actually.'

'Ski-ing?'

'No, we're going to Thailand.'

She stared at him. 'Thailand? Whatever for?'

'Well, it was Joanna's idea actually, she's always wanted to go.'

'You'll need lots of jabs,' Constance warned as she bent to kiss him. 'Well, take care, I must be off.' And she sailed towards the front door.

Which was the whole story of his mother, Dennis thought. Now you see her, now you don't.

The silver birches on the common had already turned colour and as the November winds began, the leaves drifted down, collecting in little mounds by front gates. The gardeners at Kirby Lodge and the Lutyens houses made it their priority to see

143

that the front entrances were kept immaculate. Geraniums and petunias were hauled out and winter-flowering pansies put in their place, with spring-flowering bulbs to follow.

It was around this time that Grandma Haley noticed a change in Ben. She collected him from school quite often unless another mother was going to, and his three little pals usually walked alongside him, chatting as small boys do. She listened idly at first, but after a time she concentrated more and more and heard what Ben was talking about. She became a little concerned.

'Viv,' she said to his mother – Pam had called her only daughter Vivien after seeing Vivien Leigh in *Gone with the Wind*, hoping that she would be as pretty. She almost was.

'Viv, you will have to watch Ben. He's telling fibs and making up yarns.'

'All boys do, don't they?'

'Within reason. But there's a point where the fibs become outright lies, and then they begin to believe them themselves.'

'What's he saying that's so awful?' Viv asked.

'Well,' and Pam took a deep breath, 'he tells them his father works at Cape Canaveral and is in charge of rocket launching.'

'Oh, that's rather sweet,' Viv said, smiling broadly. 'I don't see any real harm in that.'

'But he's beginning to believe it himself,' Pam said, 'and the other little chaps listen – you can see they're impressed. When that rocket launch failed, Ben said it was because they hadn't listened to his dad. The next one would be a great success because it was according to his dad's plan. He describes it in so much detail, I don't know where he gets it from.'

'Well, he went there.'

'Yes, Viv dear, but he's beginning to believe his own fantasies and that could be harmful.'

Viv sighed. 'Oh, I wish everything hadn't gone so wrong. It's ages since George wrote, and I just know...'

'What do you know?' her mother asked quietly.

'I think he's met someone else.'

'Don't be ridiculous, Viv!' Pam said sharply. 'You know no such thing, now do you?'

'I have strong suspicions,' Viv argued.

'Well, I wouldn't be surprised if there was – a wife who won't join him. You must re-member, Viv, George is a handsome young man, strong and–' she hesitated '–virile. You couldn't blame him if he did have someone although I don't for a moment believe he would, he's too fond of you and Ben.'

'So fond of us he can take himself off to the other side of the world without so much as a–'

'Now, Viv, a man has to grab hold of career opportunities these days.'

'To the exclusion of everything else? If that's not being selfish, I don't know what is.'

There was no arguing with her, Pam thought.

'You wouldn't think of emigrating?'

'No,' Viv said firmly. 'I'm British to the core and I intend to stay that way.'

Her mother sighed. It wasn't for her to judge, but it was easy to see which way the wind blew. George was a handsome man, a good catch. Other women would see it too and if one really set her sights on him George might not feel inclined to resist with his own wife being so stubborn.

'Oh, it's lovely to have you back!' Susannah cried, realising not for the first time how much she had missed them both.

'You too,' Anne said, hugging her. 'Everyone sends their love. And how is Simon?'

'Fine. He's in Scotland as I told you on the phone – back tomorrow.'

'Prospect of some business, then?' Eric asked. It was always his main preoccupation.

'Yes, hopefully. Now tell me about the trip?'

Anne decided that Susannah didn't look like a radiant bride, but after all the wedding had been some months ago and wedded bliss couldn't last forever.

Over dinner they told her of the last part of their trip which had taken them to California and very much impressed them. The lovely weather, the scenes and sights, the wonderful homes in beautiful settings.

Not until coffee was served in the drawing room did they talk about their visit to Anne's sister Felicity and their wonderful time in New York and Virginia.

'We've brought you back some presents,' Anne said. 'I can't wait for you to see them – and some for Simon.'

The nighties from New York were a joy to behold, and there was a suede jacket for Simon. 'Felicity was sure it was the right size but of course it can be exchanged.'

The evening passed so quickly.

'You are staying overnight?' Anne asked.

'Of course, Mummy.'

'Oh, good. Anyway, they all send their love.'

'How is cousin Jane?' Susannah asked finally.

'Much the same as she was here. Quiet, rides a lot, spends too much time on her own, which worries Felicity.'

'Poor Jane,' Susannah sighed.

After she had gone up to bed Anne came back downstairs into the drawing room.

'She doesn't look awfully well, does she, Eric?'

He put down his paper. 'Pining for Simon, I expect.'

'Oh, surely not? She seemed quite glad to be home. I thought she looked a bit pre-occupied.'

'Could she be – er – pregnant, do you think?' he asked.

'Possibly.' And Anne's face brightened. 'Oh, wouldn't that be wonderful?'

They were blissfully unaware that their beloved daughter was weeping back in her old bed, having discovered that yet another month had passed by without her having conceived.

George came home for Christmas armed with presents for Ben and Viv and Pam. On Boxing Day he took Ben and his friends to a football match, but somehow Ben felt it wasn't the same.

His father wasn't jolly like he used to be, and he and Mum didn't joke in the kitchen any more. They used to laugh so much once and Ben always joined in. Now it was the same as it was just before Dad had left for America. Gran took Ben on some walks to see horses in a field, and the ducks on the pond which he fed with stale bread. In fact they kept going for walks, and once a car ride in Gran's car. It seemed his parents had lots to talk about. His mother wasn't upset, she just looked cross most of the time. Every now and again she gave him a hug that hurt it was so hard.

His father left two days after Boxing Day but they didn't go with him to the airport because it was bitterly cold and the roads were icy. So he hugged Ben tightly and asked him to be a good boy and look after his mother while he was away.

After he had gone, Ben sat on the floor with his Lego. He had some wonderful Christmas presents, models of racing cars and tractors, but he still liked Lego best

149

because you could make things.

He wished Christmas had been like it used to be.

'But we'd like you to come for Christmas,' Rosemary said on the telephone. 'Really, we'd love to have you.'

'Oh, you are kind.' Barbara felt like weeping.

'Nonsense! It's ages since we've seen you, and we want to know what you've been up to. I mean it, Barbara, come to Christmas lunch and stay overnight. Of course, you'll have to drive up to town, there'll be no public transport.'

'Oh, I don't mind that,' she said.

She really would like to spend Christmas with Rosemary and her family. They had been like sisters before they'd married.

'So it's settled then? I'm really looking forward to seeing you.'

'Thanks awfully, Roz. I'll see you all then.'

Oh, what a relief! She had dreaded spending Christmas on her own. Get that over and before she knew it she would be off to India.

She still couldn't believe it.

Chapter Eight

It was a bitterly cold Sunday morning in early February when Bryan Payne left his house in Staines en route for London airport.

Well muffled up in his leather jacket and helmet, his scarf around his mouth, he started up his motor-bike and fairly roared down the street. It was only six-thirty but people were so used to Bryan's bike that they hardly heard it. He had been doing this job for over twenty years and could say in all honesty that he never got tired of it.

Next stop Delhi. He smiled in anticipation.

On the back of his bike was a parcel. He always took a pile of old clothes to India for the down and outs, kept a room in Delhi which was stacked with stuff.

The trees were covered with white frost, it certainly was a bitter morning. Difficult to think that in a few hours, less than twelve in fact, the sun would be scorching his back.

'Morning ... morning.' At Heathrow

everyone knew Bryan the Delhi courier. He parked his motor-bike, and covered it well – he wouldn't see it for another two weeks. Well wrapped up against the bitter wind, he made his way to the Terminal Three couriers' desk.

Over a hot coffee he looked at his itinerary although by now he knew it backwards.

His passengers, twelve of them, had to check in by nine for the British Airways flight to Delhi, although if they wanted special seats they would have to be much earlier for the seats were assigned on a first come, first served basis.

He knew the trip backwards. Now for the passengers. He had discovered early on that their names and addresses were no indication of what they were really like.

Twelve of them, including couples. Good, he liked couples. They looked after each other, hopefully. Single women were usually elderly and needed a bit of reassurance, especially on the Indian trip. Single men travellers he didn't go much for. Of course, there weren't many of those. Businessmen took commercial flights. Occasionally you might find a genuine bloke, one really interested in the history of India, the geographical angle – Bryan liked that. Could do with more of them. He liked to air his knowledge which was extensive. He genuinely loved the country.

There were two elderly ladies, booked into separate rooms though they were friends or relatives, almost certainly widows, both from Harrogate. A Miss Georgina Taylor, anybody's guess, from London; Mr and Mrs Leadbetter, a couple from Islington – well, he thought he knew what they would be like, either intellectuals or nouveau riche; a Dr Stevens from Bath – that was handy, always useful to have a doctor on board, that's if he were a medical man; Mrs Barbara Cooper, widow from Bucks, the name rang a bell – perhaps she had been before. He turned over the sheet to find a retired major, William Henley-Harding, and his wife. So it was the mixture as before, no young ones, they usually went backpacking. Bryan glanced at his watch. Seven-thirty. Time he got cracking.

In the special lounge assigned to them, he stood to welcome his party. A handsome man, standing head and shoulders above them all, he smiled warmly in greeting and there were many who were reassured by that.

A motley crowd, he thought, huddled up

in their lined raincoats and anoraks and scarves against the cold.

'Good morning,' he boomed, 'ladies and gentlemen, welcome to BA flight 187 to Delhi – and I don't think you will need those clothes where you are going.'

They laughed, relieved at his touch of humour. The atmosphere eased a little. They felt more comfortable with each other – and safe with him.

'Well,' he began, 'my name is Bryan Payne and I will be your escort for this tour. I hope you have your passports including valid visas for India and Nepal with you, together with any travel documents.' He glanced at his watch. 'Check-in will be no later than 9.10.' Everyone instinctively did the same.

'I have all the relevant vouchers for accommodation and tours together with the air tickets for the local flights within India and Nepal. If you have booked an extension to this tour, domestic air tickets and hotel vouchers for this extension will be issued by the hotel agency and passed on to you by me.

'Please ensure that the labels enclosed with your travel documents are attached to all items of luggage as these will help them to be recognised.

'If you have any further questions, I am at your service. In the meantime I suggest you begin to get ready for check-in.'

Barbara couldn't believe her luck. When the itinerary for the Indian trip arrived at the beginning of February, the tour manager was named as Bryan Payne, and she'd realised then how much she had hoped to see him again. There was no way of knowing when she'd booked who it would be, and she hadn't thought to ask him on that day back in the spring who he worked for. But it certainly added something to the trip to know he would be their courier.

At his announcement a great babble of conversation broke out between them and Barbara looked around with interest. To her astonishment she seemed to be one of the youngest there.

She decided to go over to Bryan Payne and re-introduce herself.

'Hello,' she said, looking up at him. He really was tall. He found himself looking down into a pair of blue-grey eyes that seemed vaguely familiar.

'Barbara Cooper,' she said, and smiled. 'You saved my life at Marylebone station.'

'I thought I recognised the name.' He

155

smiled back. 'So you decided to take my word for it and come to India?'

'Yes, I didn't need much persuading.'

'Well, here's to a good trip. And don't forget, if there's anything you're in doubt about, just ask.'

'Thank you,' she said, and moved away to join the crowd.

Another lone man, sad-looking; two middle-aged women who looked like sisters; a quiet couple, the man looking worried, the wife looking pale; a very smart woman. Well, she would get to know them all in time. Barbara was surprised herself how calm she was. She carried a lightweight plastic mac over her arm bought for sudden storms, was wearing her green suit newly pressed. Well, she wouldn't be needing these things in a few hours. She had packed the minimum amount, she thought, having really no idea. A sun hat, three cotton dresses, two cardis, slacks and shirts, one long evening shift, two pairs of sandals and some walking shoes.

'Are you on your own?' a voice asked, and she turned to find the smart-looking woman smiling at her.

'Yes, are you?'

'Have you checked in or shall we do it together? Perhaps we could sit next to each other on the plane?'

In for a penny, Barbara thought, surprising herself at her reaction. Probably because it was all like a dream and she would wake up presently.

A glance at the woman at her side showed her that here was someone who definitely would bring the right things. Not for her a boring suit. She wore narrow black trousers and a jacket, a white shirt, and her hair was cut stylishly close to her head. Her dark eyes flashed or twinkled – she used them to great effect. She carried over her arm a soft leather jacket of the most supple leather Barbara had ever seen.

'Georgie Taylor,' she said, holding out her hand. 'Well, Georgina really, but everyone calls me Georgie.'

Barbara took the proffered hand. 'Barbara Cooper.' She smiled. She's about my age, she thought, maybe a bit older, forty-fiveish. Well, she's certainly smart but she can't think I'm all that dowdy or she wouldn't have spoken to me.

'Have you been before?' she asked.

'To India? No, have you?'

'No, but I've always wanted to.'

'Me too.'

Now their little group was moving towards

check-in. Picking up her small holdall, Barbara made her way, followed by Georgie who had a much larger holdall.

'Gosh, you haven't brought much. Is that all your luggage?' she asked curiously.

'I tried to cut down on everything. I expect now I haven't brought enough.'

'Well, you can always buy out there. They say the clothes are fantastic and very cheap.' She pushed up her sleeve and looked at her arm.

'Bit of a bore all those jabs,' she said. 'My arm still hurts.'

'Does it?' They were now at the front of the queue.

'Are you going to ask for a window seat?' Georgie asked.

Barbara, who had never had to do this before for herself, looked worried.

'Well, you might prefer the aisle. If you need to – you know – get up often.'

'I don't mind,' Barbara said.

'Well, if I ask for a window seat and you sit on the aisle, is that all right?'

Barbara was happy to go along with anything, she was in such a state of euphoria.

The couple behind, his arm tightly around her, were obviously used to travel while the tall man with glasses and a frown stood

158

behind Georgie as though keeping an eye on her.

'Sorry,' he said once as he knocked her bag.

She turned brilliant eyes to him and smiled.

Barbara was so excited she thought her heart would burst. She couldn't believe she was here, actually waiting to check in on this fabulous trip to India.

Georgie got her window seat with Barbara next to her. Their luggage was checked in, leaving them only with their hand baggage.

'Coffee next, I should think, maybe a bite to eat.'

'Good idea.' Barbara was still happy to fit in with anything.

They helped themselves to coffee and croissants at the cafe and found two empty seats.

'I hope you don't mind my tagging on to you,' Georgie said. 'I just think it's nice to know who you're going to sit next to on a long plane journey.'

'This will be my longest ever,' Barbara said, breaking off a piece of croissant.

'Really?' Georgie sipped her coffee. 'I've been to the States twice.'

'How exciting. I'd love to go but India

came first.'

'You sound as if you've been waiting a long time?'

'Yes, I suppose I have really. My husband died.'

'Oh, I'm sorry.'

'It was eighteen months ago, but I'm still not used to it. We'd been married twenty years.'

'Good Lord!' Georgie seemed quite shocked by that. 'I'm on my own from choice,' she said, dark eyes suddenly brilliant.

She glanced around, and nudged Barbara.

'Over there – she's with us. Should be good for a laugh,' she whispered. 'Have you ever seen such jewellery?'

Barbara looked at the vision across the room. The woman had a mass of red hair down to her shoulders, her skin was so suntanned she looked like a wrinkled walnut, she wore masses of eye make-up and beads and gold chains, and long drop earrings, her slight bosom exposed for all to see.

'And she's no chicken,' Georgie said. 'Well, she's going to the right place, that's for sure. All that jewellery.'

And then there was a rattling of chains

beside them and the clack of high heels on the floor.

'Hi, girls!'

It was the suntanned woman, smiling broadly and showing excellent teeth. 'May I?'

'Of course.' She joined them at their table.

'Well, isn't this exciting?' she said, pulling off her gloves. 'I'm Toni Preston – Toni with an 'i' – from Preston. Isn't it a hoot? We're on the same trip, aren't we? India?'

'Barbara Cooper. And this is Georgie Taylor.'

'Either of you been before?' They shook their heads.

'Me neither,' Toni said.

At that moment an announcement came over the intercom calling the passengers for Flight 187 to assemble in the departure lounge.

They still had plenty of time, but with beating heart Barbara made her way straight there. The excitement now it had come round was almost too much to bear.

She glanced around her with interest at the other passengers now that they had all come together, and saw that Bryan was busily answering questions and checking their numbers. How reassuring to have such a capable man in charge. She felt quite relieved. The elderly couple sat huddled closely together, he still holding her arm. They looked scared stiff, she thought. While the handsome middle-aged man watched his wife anxiously, she was pale, her eyes closed. Perhaps she didn't like flying, Barbara thought.

The two lookalike ladies were expansive in more ways than one. Expensively dressed, with good jewellery and smart clothes, both were large and effusive. Toni was sitting on her own while Georgie was deep in conversation with the man with the worried expression except that now he was smiling, showing excellent teeth.

A lone elderly man was just arriving. He was tall, slim and very handsome. Sun-tanned, he looked like a diplomat or an ex-army man, Barbara thought, up to her usual trick of trying to place people. She wouldn't have thought it was his first trip to India. Perhaps he had served in the army there.

She felt the excitement mounting as the minutes ticked away, and then in what seemed to be no time at all Bryan was shepherding them through and with a great surge of excitement she walked down the ramp.

On the plane, which was newly scented and disinfected, she took her seat near Georgie by the window.

Georgie grinned, taking ages to settle herself and arrange things from her hand baggage around her just so.

They sorted themselves out, looking through the window at the frost-laden grass around London airport, and then the seat next to Barbara was taken by the man wearing glasses. The serious-eyed man, she called him.

She smiled at him.

'James Stevens,' he said. 'From Bath.'

'Barbara Cooper,' she said, 'and this is Georgie Taylor.'

Georgie nudged Barbara to look down at his small case with its label reading DR J.O. STEVENS.

'That's handy,' she whispered.

Gradually the plane filled up, and Barbara recognised several of the people from their own tour. There was much to-ing and fro-ing and sorting out of seats and luggage and clicking of seat belts, then they seemed to sit on the runway an inordinate time before the captain announced they had cleared all the delays and were about to take off.

They were moving slowly forward. Outside everything looked cold and desolate. Then all of a sudden they were airborne, leaving the ground behind them, and Barbara gulped. They were on their way.

The plane made a perfect landing at Indira Gandhi International Airport, and the first thing Barbara saw were the crowds of people on the airport roofs. Colour, colour, colour everywhere. And flowers – orange flowers, marigolds. In a dream she made her way down the gangway to greetings from women carrying garlands of flowers which were put around the necks of the new arrivals. But the heat! It hit her back like a sudden slap. All around them was heat. Like a living thing the sun beat down. It was another world.

Gathering his flock around and counting them, Bryan shepherded them through Immigration which took some time, and then to Customs, before finally arriving at the baggage reclaim. Barbara realised she had never been anywhere so foreign in her life. Beside her Georgie also seemed speechless. Soon they were in a luxury coach taking them into Delhi itself.

A short journey and the coach arrived in front of the Taj Mahal Hotel, which gleamed white and splendid, its marble steps before them, flowers everywhere and handsome young men in the uniform of the hotel just waiting to do their bidding. Once inside, the reception area seemed as big as Buckingham Palace, full of marble, and beautiful girls in saris sitting at desks anxious to help, and great bowls of roses everywhere. 'Oh!' Barbara gasped. 'Did you ever see anything so lovely?'

Bryan gathered them together. 'Now, if you will bear with me, I'll just go up to the desk and get your keys. Your rooms are ready.' And soon he returned, handing each member his or her own key.

'Now there are five restaurants in the hotel, from the very expensive luxury restaurant to the cheapest snack place which is just over there. After the journey some of you might wish to wait before sampling some of the better food. As I think I told you, watch what you eat at all times. No salads, nothing except bottled water even to clean your teeth – I can't stress that too strongly. Bottled fruit juice is OK and there are fridges in each room. So I'll hand you your keys and leave you to find your way. There's an excellent pool with many attendants – some of you might want to go for a swim – and a gymnasium. I suggest you use this evening to discover the hotel and find your way about.'

He glanced at his watch.

'We meet up in the morning after breakfast. The breakfast room is to the end of that corridor and tomorrow we shall take a coach tour. Just follow your itinerary.'

The crowd gradually dispersed to their rooms. On opening the door to hers Barbara found herself in a comfortably furnished room with a magnificent vista into the distance.

She examined the well-fitted bathroom and felt the bed and went again to the window where immediately below her on the other side of the road was what seemed to be a shanty town. High up as she was, she could only stand and stare. Flares were glowing round the hotel and even through the double-glazed windows came the smell of burning oil. There could not have been a greater contrast between the luxury of the hotel and the miserable poverty of the little shanty town on its steps.

India, she thought, that was what it was all about. She answered 'Come in' as a knock came on her door.

'Hello. I say, have you got the same view

that I have?' An astonished Georgie came over to the window to join her. 'Isn't that ghastly? You can't believe it, can you? Living like that while we're enjoying a life of luxury.'

Barbara stared into the distance. 'But look over there.' And far away they could see golden-roofed temples against a vivid dark blue sky.

Georgie turned. 'Your room is just like mine – isn't it luxurious? I can't wait to fall into that bed. When we've bathed, shall we go down and explore?'

'Love to,' Barbara said. She had lost count of the hour of the day but was determined she was going to make the most of this holiday, see if she didn't.

A short tour of the hotel soon revealed the swimming pool complex downstairs, a sauna room, a ladies' hairdresser, a gymnasium. In fact, there was nothing anyone could conceivably need that the hotel did not supply.

'Well!' George said as they made for the lift. 'I don't know about you but I'm ready for bed. See you in the morning.'

Barbara felt like a child on Christmas Eve.

Chapter Nine

Afterwards she looked back at that trip to India as being one of the best times of her life. In the morning they assembled in the coach and were driven around the streets of Delhi, making such progress as could be made through the thousands of people thronging around. They made way for bullocks and for low buses that held so many people they were falling out of windows, hanging on to the rails or sitting on the roof top. Whole families travelled on one bicycle. There were cows everywhere and men washing snowy linen in bowls at the roadside. It was truly another world.

Barbara sat next to Georgie and they alternately laughed and gasped with horror, all beneath a blazing sun and fierce heat although the coach was air conditioned.

The two women seemed to get on like a house on fire. Odd, really, considering they were such different people from very different backgrounds. But thrown together as they were, roughly of the same age, they were the only two on the tour who might conceivably become friendly. The quiet man was very retiring, as were the couples. Oh, yes, there was Toni with an 'i', but she wasn't quite Barbara's cup of tea. In another situation she and Georgie might well have ignored each other completely. Here they bonded fast.

As the coach slowed down, small boys clambered over it, knocking on windows. One enterprising woman had brought with her pencils and biros which she threw from the open windows.

'Oh, look!' from Georgie. 'That little boy – he has no arms.' And she covered her face with her hands.

'You will see horrendous sights,' Bryan said, noticing their shocked expressions. 'That's India. Nowhere in the world will you see such beauty and colour combined with such ugliness and tragedy. Some of the injuries you will see are self-inflicted or done by parents in order that the children may earn more money from tourists.'

He was a mine of information, and spoke clearly and well as they took in the old Mughal city of Delhi with its quaint bazaars, temples and mosques, going from there to the New City designed by Edwin

Lutyens, with its cool spacious avenues, parks and buildings.

'We have four houses designed by Lutyens on the common where I live,' Barbara said.

'Who's he?'

'Lutyens? The famous architect...' She broke off, laughing, as she saw that Georgie was pulling her leg.

'Our guide is good, isn't he?' Georgie observed.

'Yes, and the odd thing is I've met him before.' And Barbara told Georgie the story of her fall and how Bryan had helped her.

'Very romantic,' Georgie said, giving her a little wink. 'You could do worse.'

'Oh, don't be silly.' But Georgie noticed that she turned sharply to look out of the window.

Later that day they saw the Red Fort and Raj Ghat where a simple square platform of black marble marked the spot where Mahatma Gandhi was cremated in 1948. Afterwards to Chandni Chowk, the street of silversmiths, which was once in the richest place on earth.

'Doesn't it seem odd to see history come to life under your very eyes?' a chastened Georgie said as they sat in the medium-priced restaurant later over a meal of chicken and rice.

Bryan stopped by their table to enquire how they were getting on.

'Did you enjoy today?' he asked.

'Wonderful,' Barbara said. 'I can't wait for tomorrow – I know the days are going to fly by.'

'Enjoyable holidays always do.' He smiled. 'Now, any problems just refer them to me.' And he moved on.

'A tower of strength,' murmured Georgie. Barbara glanced swiftly at her, but her expression was blandly innocent.

The next day was a free one and they promised themselves a trip round Connaught Place to do some shopping on their own. They went by taxi, savouring the sights on the way and then browsing around the antique markets, buying small gifts that would not take up much room in their bags.

Toni joined them for coffee where she spilled out her own purchases over the table.

'Now, girls,' she said. 'What do you think? I've got a bagful down here. Look at these ... rubies, pearls, you name it. And what about this?'

She hung it around her neck to join the other necklaces and assortment of beads she habitually wore. Blue so-called sapphires and emeralds, on heavy gold chains. Bracelets such as they had never seen before.

'God,' Georgie said. 'You must have spent a fortune!'

'But a tenth of what they'd cost me at home,' she said. 'I've got an antique stall in our local hall.'

'Ah,' Georgie said, as if that explained it.

'I usually spend weekdays touting round the Indian markets – anywhere I can pick up something interesting and different – but then I thought, why not go to the source of it all? And I'm glad I did.'

'Won't you have a job getting it through Customs?'

'No, I don't think so. They're only interested in the real thing – at least, I hope so. I'll wear a lot of it. They can see the sort of lady I am.' And she winked at them.

In the afternoon they swam in the pool attended by staff who saw that their clothes were neatly folded or put on hangers and then greeted them with soft warm towels.

'This is the life,' Georgie said. 'I could get used to this.' She lay flat in a low hammock by the pool under a striped umbrella. 'Imagine, a week ago I didn't even know you existed.'

'We were lucky to meet up,' Barbara admitted.

'Where do you live?' Georgie asked idly. 'Do you have a job? What do you do?'

'Recently I've been filling in time since I lost my job in a bookshop which had to close down. I've got an Edwardian house on the edge of a common in Bucks, not far out of London. It was my in-laws' house. They left it to my husband and...'

'You stayed on there after he died?'

'Yes, it's a nice little house, I was lucky.'

'I have a flat – more of a pied-à-terre really – but it suits me. I work in London, live in London.'

'What do you do?'

'Public relations. I used to be an actress when I was younger – but, well, it's a dicey life, and I really don't think I was cut out to be an actress. But I liked the life, the uncertainty of it. When you're very young it doesn't matter. After a time, though, you ask yourself where you're going, which way are you heading. Or I did.'

Barbara waited. There was obviously a story here.

'Oh, it's all in the past. I had a long relationship. He was a handsome devil, an actor. I had a baby that died.'

'Oh, Georgie!'

'Stillborn. It happens. He walked out and I suppose I grew up. I was thirty-six and decided to do something different with my life. Anyway here I am, working in the West End, living in Bayswater.'

'You sound tough, but you must be a romantic at heart to want to come to India?'

'Yes, I suppose I am still, in a way. And I'm glad I came. I wouldn't have missed it for the world.'

Barbara looked at her through half-closed eyes. Georgie was strikingly attractive, her dark eyes almost black with long thick lashes, short shiny jet black hair inclined to curl, and smooth pale skin.

As if knowing she was under scrutiny, Georgie turned over, stood up for a moment, then dived headlong into the blue water, coming up almost at the end of the pool.

Some swimmer, thought Barbara. And what a figure.

Later they went down to the bar where James, the doctor, already sat at a corner table. He stood up as they came in.

'Ah, what have you been up to today?' he asked, looking much more relaxed now. 'What can I get you ladies to drink?'

'Let's start as we mean to go on, eh, and

pay for our own?' Georgie suggested. 'Ah, here's the waiter. For me, it's a gin and tonic – that seems to be the safest bet.'

'Me, too,' Barbara agreed.

'Can I recommend the gin sling?' James suggested.

'Oh, right, but not at the moment – we're playing safe,' Georgie laughed.

'Look, I've asked Bryan to have a meal in the second-floor restaurant. I thought I'd take it step by step and save the expensive meals until last. Will you join us?'

'Sure, nothing like some male company,' Georgie joked.

When Bryan arrived he looked quite different in his off-duty white cotton slacks and tee-shirt. Dinner was an informal affair, most of their party being in the same cool room. They found the choice limited but Bryan was able to help them order and suggest various meals.

'It's not usual to drink wine,' he said. 'It's expensive, and you soon get used to fruit juice and tonic water – which in this heat is not a bad idea.'

They were served cold soup first.

'So, how are you enjoying the trip?' he asked Barbara. He liked this quiet little woman with the cool grey-blue eyes that glowed with pleasure every time she saw something fresh.

'Oh, wonderful,' she said. 'I love every bit of it.'

'Well, tomorrow will be quite a day. We're off to Jaipur. It's one of India's most attractive cities and we shall be staying there for the next two nights. It's quite a tiring journey but worth every bit of it as I'm sure you will find when we get there.'

He pushed back his chair.

'I've some things to sort out for tomorrow so goodnight, ladies – James. See you early in the morning.'

By now they knew each one of their fellow travellers and next day greeted each other in friendly fashion as they boarded the coach for the one-hundred-and-seventy-five-mile journey to Jaipur.

There was something to see at every twist and turn. They passed a performing bear though Bryan assured them that, though once a common sight, this was now banned and very unusual. The sight of the great creature dancing on its hind legs was almost too much for the passengers in the coach. Like all Brits, they were horrified by any mistreatment of dumb animals.

'Funny, though,' Georgie whispered, 'they

don't mind seeing little boys working like slaves.'

They saw women in the fields wearing brilliantly coloured saris while picking cotton; small hovel-like towns with people sleeping on the pavements or in truckle beds outside wooden shacks. In some places women were doing the jobs of men on building sites, hods of bricks balanced on their heads or carrying cement. As they neared their destination, Bryan got to his feet.

'Jaipur is one of India's most attractive cities. On arrival you will be taken to the Rambagh Palace Hotel where we will spend the next two nights. Jaipur was planned and built by the astronomer Prince Jai Singh II, in the eighteenth century when there were few such planned cities even in Europe. It is often referred to as the Pink City because of the colour of its buildings. As you can see, it is encircled by rugged hills and crowned by mediaeval fortresses.

'It is the state capital of Rajasthan and this afternoon there will be a sightseeing tour of Jaipur which will include the Maharajah's City Palace. This is now a museum containing priceless manuscripts, ancient paintings and an armoury. You will see the observatory known as Jantar Mantar, with its huge masonry structures specifically designed for observing and collating astronomical data. And now I think we have arrived.'

The hotel resembled a film set – a beautiful building surrounded by lawns on which peacocks strutted. Tea was being served on the lawns to guests sitting in white basket chairs by waiters in long white robes. The scene was so hot, and so still, it was like a painting.

'Or something out of Merchant Ivory,' Barbara said.

The interior of the hotel was every bit as splendid. Bryan went to collect the room keys. Handing them round, he smiled when he looked at Barbara's.

'The rooms are mostly on the ground floor,' he said, 'some on the first. You are on the ground floor,' he said. 'Do you mind if I escort you? I want to show you something – you've struck lucky.'

She followed him along a corridor, cool as a spring day in England. Outside the fountains splashed, and there were flowers everywhere.

'Oh, isn't this beautiful!'

He smiled. 'May I?' She nodded as he inserted the key in the lock.

'This,' he said, 'was the original apothecary's room – you are very fortunate.'

She looked at the huge bed. Everywhere was painted dark blue and red while from the ceiling swung an enormous four-bladed fan. There were huge armchairs and exquisite pieces of furniture inlaid with mother-of-pearl and silver.

'Oh, but it's beautiful,' she gasped. 'I never saw such a room.'

'The luck of the draw,' he whispered, and left her to revel in it.

She opened the door to the immense bathroom with its cool interior, a big white bath and twin basins.

Oh, that this holiday could last forever!

There was a knock on the door and she opened it to find Georgie standing there, open-mouthed as she glimpsed the interior of Barbara's room.

'Golly!' she said. 'Is this all yours?'

Barbara grinned at her.

'Talk about favouritism!' her friend said. 'I'm on the next floor.'

'It's the original apothecary's room,' Barbara found herself whispering.

'Well, I'm not surprised. You know, I'll bet he engineered this. He's taken a fancy to you.'

'Who? The apothecary?'

'No! Bryan – our Bryan – he's obviously got a soft spot for you.'

'Oh, don't be so ridiculous!' Barbara said, her cheeks flaming.

Georgie sank down on to the bed with its jewel-coloured quilt while Barbara walked to the window.

'Peacocks strutting on the lawn, what a sight,' she sighed.

'And what a noise they'll make,' Georgie said. She was nothing if not practical.

The next morning they were driven seven miles to the deserted city of Amber, which was once the capital before Jaipur was founded in 1727. On top of a hill over-looking the city was the Amber Palace. The entrance to the great courtyard was through an arched gateway and when Bryan announced that those of them who wanted to could ride up to the palace on an ele-phant, both Barbara and Georgie opted for it.

'Couldn't bear to miss an opportunity like this!' Georgie cried.

The elephants were huge, with painted faces, and each howdah held four people, sitting in pairs back to back. A *mahout* helped them to climb the small ladder.

They giggled and laughed, but were really a trifle scared. Barbara found it most uncomfortable, and had the awful feeling she was going to fall off whenever the elephant took a lumbering step. To ease the tension they laughed like children at the little monkeys scrambling about in the trees, waiting for visitors to throw them food.

The Temple of Kali had silver-plated doors and was faced with beautiful marble-work. There was also a Palace of Mirrors whose ceilings and walls had mosaics and inlays of glass – it was difficult to absorb so much beauty at one time.

Once down on terra firma again they saw the five-storey Palace of the Winds with its overhanging windows behind which there was reputedly nothing.

Long after she had gone to bed Barbara lay awake trying to make the most of this extraordinary holiday. The soft whirr of the fan finally lulled her to sleep.

Over breakfast, Bryan announced that today they would be going to Agra, the capital of the Mughal Empire and a Mecca for all tourists.

There, he said, they would see the Taj Mahal, the most perfect example of Mughal architecture. It had been built by the Emperor Shah Jahan in 1652 to enshrine the remains of his wife, Mumtaz Mahal. It was a long drive, first one hundred and twenty-five miles to the ghost city of Fatehpur Sikri, twenty-three miles from Agra. They would make a short detour to a bird sanctuary before arriving at Fatehpur Sikri.

'The history of this place goes back to the sixteenth century and the entire fortress city is built of red stone,' Bryan said. 'A famous mystic spent his days meditating in a grotto in this little community of stone cutters, and legend grew up around him. Word came to the Emperor Akbar who set out on a pilgrimage to ask the holy man for the blessing of an heir. When a son was born the king named him after the mystic and decided to move his capital to Sikri. Within five or six years a complex of forts, palaces and mosques sprang up. However, because of the shortage of water, Akbar was forced to abandon his new capital and today it is haunted by the memories of a once resplendent era. A true ghost city.'

'You can see how he loves all this,' Georgie whispered.

'Well, it's his life,' Barbara said.

'We will now continue on to Agra and you will be transferred to the Shiraz Hotel where we will spend the next two nights.'

'Oh,' Barbara sighed, 'I can't believe any of this – it's even more wonderful than I imagined.'

'Me too,' said Georgie.

When the coach stopped and the Taj Mahal stood before them in all its magnificent splendour, unbelievably white against the green lawns, looking like a gigantic film set, it was a very emotional moment for most of them.

'The Mecca for all tourists,' Bryan said. 'It took twenty-two years to create this jewel, and inside you will find delicate inlay work of precious stones in marble, and the mausoleum enshrines all that is most tender in a man's love for a woman.'

Barbara felt herself come out in goose pimples and felt quite carried away. They could only stand and wonder as at last it stood before them, the long dreamed of sight. Barbara's eyes filled with tears. She sat down for a while on a nearby seat before walking up the path towards it. She walked alone, leaving her own little crowd. She wanted to be quiet with her own thoughts.

Behind her walked James and Georgie, she

too overcome with such emotion she could hardly speak.

As they approached the shrine they took off their shoes and left them at the door, as they had done for most of the religious shrines they had seen.

Bryan joined them to describe some of the workmanship then walked over to Barbara.

'Hard to describe your feelings, isn't it? I've seen it hundreds of times and I always feel the same. You never get used to it – it is literally beyond belief.'

'I feel I'm so lucky to have seen it,' Barbara said, blowing her nose. 'It takes your breath away.'

James walked with Georgie, both of them deep in thought, while Toni insisted on having her photograph taken sitting in just the same position as Princess Diana. She sat bedecked in jewels, her hair a tumble of red-brown and blonde. Her earrings nearly reached her shoulders and she kept her head tilted slightly to one side in what she probably considered a captivating pose.

'How old do you think she is?' Georgie whispered.

'I have a doctor's professional etiquette to consider.' James smiled. 'Older than you, certainly.'

They spent some time inside absorbing as much as they could – it was a feast for the eyes. Later, much later, they walked back to the coach.

'Now, I think we shall make for some cool drinks.'

Nearby there was a stall dispensing bottled drinks beneath the shade of a huge tree. Cows roamed free, and two oxen pulled a grass cutter.

'Phew! It's hot,' Georgie said, mopping her face and putting her sun hat back on.

'Is it your first visit to India?' James asked, sitting down at her side.

'Yes, and I'm completely overwhelmed. What about you?'

'Yes, me too. I've always promised myself this trip.'

'Hard to find the time, I expect?'

'That's true,' he said. 'My first break for three years – proper break, that is.'

'Are you a medical doctor?' she asked.

'Yes, a GP. I've a practice in Bath. I should say, I share a practice with three others.'

'Bet that keeps you busy.'

'What about you?'

'I live and work in London,' Georgie said. 'Ah, here's Barbara.'

'Well, I think I've managed to pull myself

together – quite shattering, isn't it?'

'You can say that again,' Georgie agreed.

'Well,' Bryan said, joining them, 'I think it's time we made tracks. Get you back to the hotel in time to freshen up before dinner.'

He smiled at Barbara then went over to her.

'Quite an experience, isn't it?'

'Emotionally, yes,' she said. 'Such a love story.'

Their eyes held for a moment, then he checked the rest of the group.

'Right, that's it, back to the coach.'

'The hotel has two good restaurants,' Bryan told them.

'Take your choice and be up bright and early for the flight to Khajuraho where we will spend one night before our flight to Varanasi. Everyone comfortable? Good. Off we go.'

Chapter Ten

Still sated with the memory of the Taj Mahal, the small group of tourists were subdued on the short flight to Khajuraho, fascinated by the beautiful stewardesses in saris who offered them boiled sweets on the plane. When they arrived at the airport a coach drove them to the Chandella Hotel where they would spend the night.

That afternoon they would visit the temples with their erotic carvings. A thousand years ago the robust Chandella warriors had lived, loved and triumphed, and having reached the peak of their power, built temples to their gods with all the fervour of a virile race.

Bryan's group were struck dumb by this fine example of mediaeval Indian art. It happened every time, he thought. Whether it was a reaction to seeing the Taj Mahal and its beauty the previous day, or genuine shock and disbelief at some of the carvings which depicted griffins, nymphs, beasts and mortals caught in every human emotion, fear, doubt, jealousy, ardent love and consummated passion, the sight reduced them to silence. You needed more than half a day to appreciate this place, he thought privately, and doubted whether most of his tour understood it. After twenty years he was still in awe of it.

'Tomorrow morning,' he announced, 'you will be taken from your hotel to the airport at Khajuraho in time for the flight to Varanasi.'

'You mean, there's more?' asked Georgie.

It was a forty-minute flight to Babatpur Airport then they were transferred to the Taj Ganges Hotel where they were to spend the night.

'Now it will be an early start,' Bryan explained, 'and if you would rather not, say so now then I won't have to wait for you, but we leave early in order to see the dawn rise over the Ganges.'

There was a slight groan, but everyone knew this was one of the highlights of the tour.

They walked through countless alleyways and byways, the streets thronged with pilgrims. Though it was still not yet light, a strange air that hung about the place affected them all.

Bryan explained as they went along.

'It used to be known as Benares, which some of you will remember, famous for its brassware and silks. It sprawls along the left bank of the River Ganges. It is the most ancient occupied city in the world. It is also the holiest city in India, and dates back long before 500Bc when Buddha first visited the settlement. To millions of Hindu devotees it is the most sacred place of pilgrimage in their religion. They go there to bathe in the River Ganges and to worship at the shrine of Vishwanath. Bathing in the River Ganges is considered to be one of the most important things a Hindu can do, and each morning thousands perform the ritual on the banks.'

It became lighter as they walked, and there was an unearthly sepia colour overhanging everything. It grew hot as time wore on, and then there it was – the River Ganges, with the golden-red sun rising out of the water. A cold shudder ran down many spines. Barbara felt strangely emotional at the sight, near to tears that it should come to life before her very eyes. There they were, hundreds of pilgrims, innumerable shrines, temples and palaces rising in tiers through the haze, as if caught in a time warp.

'The goal of every Hindu pilgrim is to die here,' Bryan said, 'so that his or her ashes may be scattered on the river.'

There was not a sound from anyone in his group.

'Now, we have a small boat so that we may see this wonderful view at its best.'

They climbed in and took their seats, seeing the burning ghats and cremation ceremonies, while at the same time at the dhobi ghats men and women did their washing. The view from the boat was breathtaking.

Bryan explained about the men carrying planks of wood and branches to start fires on which would be placed the dead body of their relative.

'Somehow it all makes sense when you are here,' Barbara said, overcome with awe at the sight of it all. As the sun rose, so did the heat, and for her this was the most magical part of the whole trip, even surpassing the view of the Taj Mahal.

It was a very subdued crowd who made their way back to the hotel for breakfast, after which they were transferred to the airport for the flight to Kathmandu.

The sight of Mount Everest, although its peak was shrouded in mist, was breathtaking and Bryan informed them that those who wished could take a separate flight to see the mountain, weather permitting.

Barbara and Georgie decided to wait and see what happened in Nepal. Once they arrived, there was quite a long procedure to go through at Customs and Immigration.

Barbara was not sure what she had expected of Nepal, but it was as unlike India as she could have imagined. The hotel proved to be a luxurious place with a swimming pool and sports complex, and there was evidence everywhere in the main streets of hippy communes – there were modern buildings alongside ancient pagodas and statues.

They were to spend three days here, to unwind or go on optional excursions.

They relaxed and later some of them spent the afternoon and evening exploring the local shops and the town which was crowded with visitors.

In the big market square, ringed with pagoda-like structures, Bryan opened his haversack before a waiting crowd who fell on its contents of trousers, tee-shirts and sweaters. They obviously awaited his arrival with great enthusiasm.

In one square they looked up at a window where the Goddess Kali might be seen on special occasions, and there she was: a little girl of five or so, her face painted with the most exotic make-up.

'It is considered a great honour to be chosen to represent Kali,' Bryan told them. 'The competition is fierce with thousands of aspirants, and once chosen she lives the life of a recluse – never coming into the outside world, waited on hand and foot. You occasionally see her appear at that small window – we were lucky today. It's months since I last saw her, and this one is new.'

The tiny face at the window with its kohl-ringed eyes surveyed them with an unblinking stare.

'How long is she there for?' whispered Georgie.

'Until she arrives at puberty. Then she is considered unclean and a new goddess is found.'

'How absolutely barbaric!' Georgie said. 'I've never heard anything so disgusting!'

Their small group was glad to move on past the wonderfully painted pagodas and golden buddhas – there was so much to see in this colourful country.

Back at the hotel, they elected to go for a swim in the pool, and afterwards lay resting before dinner.

'Tomorrow we shall go for a long walk if

you feel you are up to it.' And Bryan set out the details.

It was a beautiful morning, not too hot, as they set out from the hotel. By now everyone in the party knew everyone else and had paired off. They went first to a Tibetan commune where women sat on the floor sewing and embroidering, and they were offered small biscuits and green tea.

Afterwards they were free to wander at will over the countryside where hills rose in the distance and the sparse vegetation sometimes gave way to a stand of trees or a patch of wild flowers.

As Georgie walked ahead with James, Bryan caught up with Barbara.

'Are you enjoying it?' he asked. 'Does it come up to your expectations?'

'Oh, it exceeds them,' she replied. 'It has been absolutely wonderful. I don't wonder that you enjoy your work. I shall really be sorry when this ends.'

'Then you must come again, perhaps see some other places. Rajasthan is wonderful, although it has changed somewhat and you would have to go at the right time of the year.'

He pointed. 'Just thirty miles over there lies Tibet.'

Barbara stared into the distance at the furrowed land which dipped towards them, then caught sight of a wild rose bush covered in white flowers. There was no one to be seen for miles around.

'Oh! Look at that – white roses!' And from out of nowhere a small brown boy came running up to her, holding out a single white bloom.

Barbara stared at him, then at Bryan.

'Where did he come from? How could he know what I said?'

Bryan smiled. 'They're everywhere,' he said. 'Take it – he wants money.' And he fished in his pocket, pulling out a coin.

The boy gave a wide grin and disappeared back the way he'd come.

'Well,' Barbara said, looking down at the rose. She knew she would keep it long after it had faded.

They found a cool grassy patch under a tree, and sat down.

'You really have enjoyed it?' Bryan repeated.

'Yes, really, and you have been wonderful. We couldn't have asked for a better guide.'

'Thank you,' he said. 'It's easy for me, it's my second home.'

'And you always come to the same places?'

'Mostly. Sometimes if another guide is ill or away I do their trip, but it's usually the same one.'

'I can't wait to tell my friends about this,' Barbara said, arms around her knees. The scent from the flowers was enhanced by the hot sun.

'You must persuade them all to come too,' he said.

'I can't bear to think of going home. It will be so dull after this. Still, holidays can't last forever.'

'What do you do?' he asked her.

'I've been filling in time with voluntary work, but when I get back I shall look for another permanent job.'

'You miss your husband, I expect,' he said, noticing the wedding ring. 'I understand you are a widow?'

'Yes, William died almost two years ago.'

'My wife died ten years ago from cancer.'

'Oh, I'm sorry. How awful.'

'Yes, it was. Still, I have a daughter. She's recently married so now she's moved away, I'm on my own.'

'Its hard to get used to, isn't it?' Barbara asked.

'Well, I'm away so much, I hardly have time to notice.'

Lucky man, she thought.

'You live in Bucks, don't you?'

'On the edge of a common.'

'I'm in Staines, convenient for the airport.'

Bryan stole a sideways glance. He saw her dark hair beneath her sun hat, the sunglasses hiding her clear eyes, the smooth unlined skin, the resolute chin – surprising in someone so gentle, he thought, for want of a better word. Barbara was quite unlike the other woman she had teamed up with. But then, these trips were always an eye opener. They brought about the most unlikely pairing off of singles, of disparate people with only one thing in common: they'd wanted to visit the same places.

He had made many friends on these trips, some he still kept in touch with, nice women, friendly women, but there was something about Barbara Cooper that held a special appeal. Perhaps because, he told himself, he had first met her in very different circumstances.

He hesitated, then turned to face her.

'I expect you come to London sometimes – after all, that's where we first met, isn't it?' And he smiled.

What nice eyes he has, she thought. Kind eyes.

'Yes, sometimes. I have a friend in London, an old school friend.'

'Could we meet for lunch one day?' he said. 'I know quite a few restaurants in the Marylebone area – near your station.'

Barbara's heart leapt. A date!

'Yes, I'd like that,' she said.

He took out a diary.

'Well, it's either next week or three weeks' time. You say.'

'Better make it in three weeks' time,' she said, surprised at herself.

'We'll talk about it later,' he said. 'Now I must see what everyone else is up to.' And he got to his feet. 'It's like rounding up lost sheep. I hope no one's disappeared. Don't want them ending up in the wilds of Mongolia...'

He helped Barbara to her feet and she felt again the reassurance of a strong hand on hers as she had that day when she'd stumbled back in London.

Oh, it would be nice to have something to look forward to.

She knew she was going to find it difficult to settle back at home after a trip like this.

Three days later, after clearing Immigration and Customs once again, they boarded the

plane for the airport in Delhi, being transferred to the Taj Mahal Hotel for their last
night. They all joined forces for a slap up
meal in the most expensive restaurant,
joined by Bryan, everyone making promises
to meet again which most of them would
not keep.

Barbara noticed that Georgie was getting
on famously with James, and although they
seemed an unlikely pair she knew her friend
was interested in him.

Later she came to Barbara's room for a
nightcap and they went over all they had
seen and done since arriving two weeks ago.

'Can't bear to think it's over,' Georgie
sighed. 'London is going to feel very dull
after this.'

'Are you going to see James again?'
Barbara asked casually.

'Yes, he's asked me to meet him in London when he comes for a medical conference in March. He's awfully nice, Barbara.
Not at all like the men who usually attract
me. He's different. Because he's a doctor, I
suppose. I don't usually care for the public
relations type but that's my world so I don't
meet many other men. What about you and
Bryan?'

Barbara didn't colour up this time, merely

lipsticked her mouth. 'New colour – nice?'

'Suits you. I wondered what you were making up for just before going to bed.' And Georgie gave a little laugh.

Barbara wiped off the lipstick with a tissue.

'I wasn't exactly blind to the friendship which seemed to spring up between you and Bryan,' Georgie probed, examining her nails.

'He's asked me to meet him for lunch in town.'

'And will you?'

'Yes, why not? It's ages since I had lunch with a man. Well, apart from on this trip, I mean.'

'By the way, I hope we don't lose touch,' Georgie said, and Barbara knew she meant it.

'Of course not. Why should we?'

'Could I come down to see you?' Georgie asked. 'You know, for lunch, dinner, whatever?' She rummaged in her handbag and brought out a card. 'Give me a ring. Now don't forget.'

'And here's mine,' Barbara said, writing her address and telephone number down on a sheet of hotel notepaper.

Georgie folded it and put it in her handbag, going over to the window and looking down at the burning flares of the encampment below. 'Still there,' she said. 'It does seem awful, doesn't it? Well, I suppose we can say we've seen a little bit of India.'

'From quite the nicest hotels,' Barbara said. 'Still, I'm grateful for what I've seen and not unaware of the poverty all around. How could you hide from it in India?'

Georgie looked wistful. 'Some things we'll never forget, will we? They're imprinted on our minds.'

Barbara came to join her at the window and watched the flares in the dark. By the moonlight she could make out the golden domes on the horizon.

'It's looks magical.'

'You can almost smell the burning oil from here,' Georgie said, ever practical. 'Well, I'm for bed. 'Night, Barbara.'

''Night, Georgie.'

But long after she had gone to bed, Barbara lay awake thinking of Bryan and his invitation to lunch.

The plane trip home was uneventful. Everyone seemed subdued, and it seemed to pass quickly.

'Wonder what the weather's like in England?' Georgie said. 'Still cold, I expect.'

'All that lovely Indian sunshine,' Barbara sighed. 'Back home it will be heating on, boiler going.'

'Did you bring a car to the airport?' Georgie asked.

'No, I was given a lift by a neighbour but I'll get a taxi back. How about you?'

'I'll get a train to Paddington.'

'I never thought of that.'

Once clear of Customs they made their way to the exit, no one more surprised than Barbara to see Viv waiting for her in the Arrivals hall.

Barbara hurried towards her and threw her arms about her. 'Oh, Viv, how wonderful! How did you know?'

'Phoned Arrivals and they told me. Oh, you look wonderful!'

Barbara took a deep breath.

'I feel wonderful,' she said. 'It was the most fabulous trip, you can't imagine.'

'I'm pleased,' Viv said. 'I worried about you.'

'You needn't have,' Barbara said. 'Where's Ben?'

'At my mother's.'

By their side stood Georgie, patiently waiting.

Barbara turned. 'Oh, Georgie, I'm sorry. Viv, meet Georgie – we travelled together.'

They both shook hands.

And then there was Bryan, hurrying towards them, raincoat over his arm, knapsack on, carrying his cap.

'Thought I'd missed you.' And he smiled down at the three women.

'Viv, this is Bryan Payne. Bryan – my neighbour Viv McKay.'

'How do you do?' He nodded. 'So you have an escort home.' He smiled at Barbara. 'What about you, Georgie?'

'Going to Paddington,' she said.

'Well, I'll be off,' he said, putting on his cap. 'Ladies.' And he was gone, making for the car park where he kept his motor-bike.

'Who was that?' Viv asked.

'You may well ask.' Georgie grinned.

Chapter Eleven

Viv brought the car to a standstill outside Barbara's house.

'Now, look, when you've unpacked and had a little rest, come round to us. Ben will be back later – about six thirty–'

'Oh Viv,' Barbara said. 'You don't have to...'

'I've already got dinner prepared. You'll need a hot meal after your trip. Besides, Ben wants to hear all about India and the elephants – you did see an elephant, I hope?'

'I rode an elephant,' Barbara said with a grin.

'That settles that, then,' Viv said, getting out of the car and unlocking the boot.

'Come when you're ready – anytime to suit you...'

'Oh, you are a dear,' Barbara said. Bright eyed, she looked up at her home.

An empty house, she thought, then straightened her shoulders, and picking up her suitcase made for the front door. She found her keys and went inside.

There was always an unlived-in smell to a house that had been shut up. She wrinkled her nose, experiencing again that awful sensation of being quite alone in the world. She wanted William to be there, almost felt like calling his name – William, I'm home. Oh, you can't believe what I've seen, where I've been.

But there was nothing but silence. Dropping her luggage, Barbara picked up the pile of letters, and took them with her through to the living room. She opened the curtains wide and looked out at the garden. Daffodil spears pierced the ground, defying the wintry scene of bare trees and bushes, while a few polyanthus flowered brilliantly in a large pot. She swallowed hard.

Home!

Before doing anything else, she switched on the central heating and ran the cold water tap for a spell, touching the radiators automatically. The houseplants she had left in the sink seemed to have grown in the two weeks she had been away.

She went upstairs and pulled back the curtains in her bedroom – hers and William's – unable to believe that for the last thirteen nights she had slept in various beds in an exotic country called India...

Looking at herself in the bathroom mirror, she saw that she was faintly tanned, although she had not consciously been trying to. She looked well, she could see that. Rested, the frown lines smoothed away. She went downstairs to put the kettle on to make tea, then began to open the post.

There were bills, naturally and unsolicited mail – plenty of that – envelopes telling her to look inside immediately as she had won thousands of pounds, but she didn't open those. They went straight into the bin. One from Mrs Pargetter-Wilson reminding her of the coffee morning in aid of sick children. It was to be held just before Easter – she would go to that. There was also a postcard from the library telling her about an overdue book...

She filled a hot water bottle, made a cup of tea and took both upstairs to bed. The sheets were icy but half undressed, she slipped into bed, grateful for the bottle. She was soon asleep.

She woke at five thirty feeling refreshed, the cup of tea cold beside her. She leapt out of bed, thinking she had time for a bath and change of clothes before going to Viv's.

What a difference it had made to her life,

her friendship with Viv. To be picked up and welcomed home was indeed a gift from the gods.

It was just after six thirty when, bathed and changed, and armed with Viv's present – a picture painted on silk – and a small colourful elephant and the model of an Indian bus for Ben, she rang the bell of Viv's house.

'Ah, that's better,' Viv said 'you looked exhausted. Was everything all right? I kept an eye on the house–'

'I'm sure you did, thanks,' Barbara smiled, and gave her the small square package.

Ben came running out of the kitchen with shining eyes. 'Hello, Barbara.'

'And this is for you,' Barbara said. 'I hope you like it.'

He was fascinated by the small elephant.

'Do they paint the real elephants?' he asked.

'Only the ones that give rides,' Barbara said. 'I had a ride on one, and it was beautifully painted, its ears and its face.'

He was open mouthed. 'Is that cruel?' he asked.

'No, I don't think they mind – they paint a lot of things in India,' Barbara said.

'How about a gin and tonic?' Viv asked. 'A

welcome home drink as it were?'

'Lovely,' Barbara said, already missing the crowd she had been with in India and their pre-dinner drinks.

Armed with drinks, they sat in the small comfortable lounge.

'Well – how was it? Come up to expectations?'

'More than that – it was wonderful, absolutely wonderful.'

Viv, who quite genuinely could not understand anyone's desire to visit India, was prepared nevertheless to listen to Barbara's tales.

'Wild horses wouldn't get me there,' she said. 'I haven't the slightest interest in it, nor the Orient.'

'Nor even America,' Barbara said with a smile.

'Yes. I'm just not a traveller. Now my mother has been half way round the world – if she could travel free she'd be off tomorrow. Only money stops her going.'

'Well, India was my particular wish,' said Barbara, 'and I could go again tomorrow–'

Viv got up. 'Hold on – just need to check on dinner. It's roast lamb, mint sauce and apple pie,' she said. 'Mum made the pie and sends her love.'

'Oh, wonderful!' Barbara said. She was

looking forward to it after the food on the trip, which had not been a gastronomic experience.

'So, tell me about the people on the trip?'

'Well, first of all, there was the guide, Bryan.'

'The man at the airport? He was your guide? Oh, boy…'

'Yes. You remember the man who helped me at Baker Street that day when I fell – who started this whole thing off? Well, that was Bryan.'

'And you didn't know?' Viv was sceptical.

'Of course I didn't, not until they sent the itinerary a week or so before we left – and he was marvellous. Wonderful at his job – he's been doing it for twenty years…'

The time flew as Barbara described some of the people from the trip.

'What about Georgie – the girl I met? She looked interesting.'

'We teamed up – she works in public relations and lives in Bayswater – it worked very well. I couldn't imagine it when we first met, but we became friends – really because we were about the same age and both on our own. There were several couples, and two elderly sisters – oh, and an odd bod – an older lady – about seventy. You know, Viv, it was so good to meet someone like Georgie, it would have been really miserable if she hadn't been there–'

'Even with Bryan there?'

'Well, he had a job to do – oh, it was such fun, Viv!'

'Well, you're looking bloomin' marvellous – so relaxed.'

Barbara caught a note of envy. 'But enough about me – how are you? And George? How is he getting on?'

Viv glanced down at the floor where Ben was playing. 'Still in Florida. Things aren't improving – not in that direction, anyway. I'll tell you later – and something else, too.'

The meal Barbara had to admit was the best she had eaten for two weeks.

After Ben had been tucked in and Viv had read him a story, Viv came downstairs.

'I nearly forgot,' she said. 'Your bookshop – the one you worked in in Texbury – is re-opening.'

'Really? What as?'

'A bookshop – can you believe it? There is a notice in the window – interesting, isn't it? Perhaps you could get your old job back?'

'I don't know that I want it – except that I have to get a job of some sort. I wonder who has taken it over?'

'No idea. Perhaps you could find out more tomorrow?'

'Yes, I'll get cracking on it. Now what did you have to tell me? I thought you seemed a little excited.'

'Not really – except that I met this guy.'

'Oh,' Barbara still had hopes of George and Viv getting back together.

'Don't be like that. He's nice – I went out for a meal with him the other evening. He's divorced and his name's Jim. Mum looked after Ben for the evening.'

Barbara waited.

'And you like him?'

'Yes, he's a sales rep. An ex-footballer–'

'Golly.'

'Well, briefly. I've asked him round next Saturday. After all, Barbara, there is no reason why I shouldn't have boy friends, is there? I'm sure George is having the time of his life over there–'

'You might be imagining that, Viv, But after all, you're both young–'

'Oh, come on, you sound like my mother. Tell me some more about this Bryan bloke?'

'Not much to tell. He's a widower, has been for ten years, got a newly married daughter.'

'How old is he?'

'About fifty, I should think–'

'And you liked him – not just as a guide, I mean?' She saw Barbara's cheeks redden.

'Well, that's great,' she said. 'Let's hope you see him again – are you going to?'

'He asked me to meet him in town for lunch one day.'

'And will you?'

'Yes, of course – I'm looking forward to it.'

The following Saturday, after lunch, Viv stood with her back to the sink having cleared away the dirty dishes. Wiping her hands with the small towel, she examined her nails.

'By the way, Ben, I've asked a friend round this afternoon – I thought we might go for a walk ... and perhaps have tea out?'

'What's her name?'

'It's a man,' Viv said.

'A friend of Dad's?'

'No – someone from the office,' Viv said. 'His name is Peter – Peter Walker–'

Ben went on playing.

When the doorbell rang, Viv went to answer it, giving a last glance at her hair in the hall mirror.

'Hi, Peter,' she said. 'Come in, come and meet Ben.' Ben sat on the floor in the kitchen with his toys. 'This is Peter, Ben; Peter, my son,' Viv said.

Ben stood up and studied Peter gravely. Well, he wasn't much to look at, not very tall, but well built, broad shoulders, nothing in the least like his dad, who had been good looking, tall and slim. Peter also had a bit of a limp. Disappointment ran through Ben. Was this going to be his new dad? Lots of boys had new fathers and they sometimes didn't like who they got. But Peter looked kind, even if he did limp, and his mother seemed to like him.

'Do you like Lego?' he asked Peter suspiciously.

'Sure.' Peter said, squatting down on the floor with him, which was a good start.

Viv stood back again by the sink.

'Peter used to be a footballer,' she said.

'Well, not strictly, Viv.' Peter said. 'I was in the first reserves, until I broke my leg.'

'Yes, that was bad luck,' she said.

'Who's your favourite team?' Ben asked.

'Arsenal,' Peter said. 'No two ways about it.'

'Arsenal!' Ben cried. 'That's mine, too–'

'I played for Arsenal,' Peter said. 'I might have been really good if I hadn't broken my leg, but that's the luck of the draw.'

'Arsenal!' shrieked Ben. Wait until he told the others.

Later on, Peter took him to play football and bought him an Arsenal tee-shirt for his birthday.

'My mum's got a new boy friend,' he told his mates. 'He's an Arsenal footballer,' and waited for it to sink in.

'What?' they shrieked. 'What's his name?' and Ben realised he was being put to the test.

'Well, he was until he broke his leg – otherwise he'd be famous. He still plays on Saturdays. He bought me an Arsenal shirt.'

'What about your real dad?' one of them asked. 'Does that mean we won't know about the rocket launchings?'

''Course not,' he said. 'I expect he'll be writing to me any day now – I'm waiting for a letter. He might be home for Easter...'

But somehow, he didn't really think he would.

Viv's mother took her Easter card to the post office to have the correct postage put on it. It was addressed to George McKay in Florida, America.

There were bunny rabbits on the card and daffodils flowering in a sunny English village, and inside she had written a note.

Dear George,
Thank you for the card from Washington. It looks very nice. We are all O.K. Little Ben's school has broken up for Easter. Viv's neighbour, Barbara, is back from India, and Viv has a new friend. His name is Peter – a nice chap. Ben gets on with him. He comes round to dinner sometimes and takes Ben to football matches. He misses his dad.

Hope you are well, George. Don't work too hard.

Love Pam.

There was a man working inside the closed bookshop. Barbara could see him quite clearly even through the whitewashed window. She knocked on the window a few times before another man came to the door and opened it.

'Yes?'

'Um, I hope you don't mind my calling, but I understand that you are re-opening the bookshop. I'm Barbara Cooper...'

'Yes?' the man said. He wore glasses and was about forty-five with a thin face and a shock of dark hair.

'It's just that – are you the owner?'

'Not exactly. I'm leasing the premises, but... Can I help you?' He seemed to relax a little.

'It's just that I used to work here,' Barbara said somewhat lamely, 'and I wondered...'

'Oh,' he visibly brightened. 'Come in,' he said.

She walked into the once familiar surroundings, now being painted dark green by a young painter, while she could see the office was now a deep cardinal red. That'll cheer the place up, she thought.

'Sorry I can't ask you to sit down,' he said. 'Um—'

'That's all right,' Barbara said. 'I suppose – will you be needing staff?'

'Well, I hope so,' and he suddenly gave a boyish grin, 'I mean it depends on the business – look, can I take your name and telephone number? Do you live locally?'

'Yes, quite near,' Barbara said. 'Here is my name and address and number and if you do decide that you need someone to help out, perhaps you would give me a ring?'

'I shall know better after I've opened,' he said, 'which should be in about two weeks – I should warn you that it wouldn't be full time.'

'Oh, that wouldn't matter ... Is it to be a

general bookshop, like it was before? Or–'

'Oh, yes,' he said.

They seemed to have reached an impasse.

'Well,' Barbara said. 'I mustn't hold you up...'

He held out his hand. 'I'm Tim,' he said. 'Tim Riley.'

She took it. 'Well, er, Mr Riley, I hope to hear from you.'

I wonder, she thought, walking home. Can he make more of a success of it than Janet did? Or had Janet just got bored having had the shop for so long. She had come to a retirement age, anyway, and since the closing had come so soon after William's death Barbara had no alternative but to leave.

We'll see, she thought happily. I shouldn't mind going back there, after all, it's a business I know.

Three weeks later she met Bryan at Marylebone station after having coffee with Rosemary, who wanted to hear all about the Indian trip. She had taken a taxi to the station and now it was almost one o'clock.

Bryan looked a little different, dressed as he was in a lounge suit. Quite a city gentleman, she thought, and found she was

216

more than pleased to see him again.

They fell into an easy stride. Like a pair of old friends, she thought, happy to be in his company.

He took her to a small restaurant nearby where they had a glass of wine each and sat looking at each other across the table.

They ordered soup and salads, and sat back to await their food. He has nice eyes, Barbara thought. It was one of the first things she had noticed about him.

'Well, I suppose you've done another trip to India since we last met,' she said. 'Did anything exciting happen?'

'One of the elderly ladies fell and was badly bruised but that didn't seem to deter her, she was positive she wanted to resume the tour. She must have been in some pain. Anyway she insisted on joining us the next morning, otherwise it was pretty much the same as before – but what about you?'

'Well, it was a bit grim settling back in after all the excitement.' She paused.

The waitress brought their soup.

'Something interesting has happened,' Barbara said. 'I think I told you I used to work in a bookshop which closed down? Well, it is re-opening, and I called in and asked if there was any chance of a job–'

Bryan raised his brows. 'Is that what you want?'

'Not really, but I have to do something – and I have had experience of the book world. Anyway, he doesn't know yet if he will need staff, so we will have to see.'

She finished her soup. 'How is your daughter?'

'I went to dinner the night before I left for India. She seems very happy. Between you and me, Barbara, I have a feeling she might be pregnant–'

'And you'll be a grandfather...' She smiled, then met his eyes.

'Could you accept that – a lunch date with a grandfather?'

Barbara laughed out loud. 'Oh, Bryan! You would be so lucky – I wish I'd had children...' Her voice tailed away, and she felt herself flushing, for some reason embarrassed.

Hastily she crumbled her bread.

'After your next trip, Bryan, would you like to come down for Sunday lunch? To Birch Common? It'll be a lovely time of the year, the garden will look nice. It's quite small, but pretty, and we could take a walk... I could pick you up from the station–' She stopped, wondering if he would think her too pushy.

She was astonished at her bravery, but then when you reached a certain age, you could do things like this. Young people today thought nothing of it. She heard her mother's voice. 'Always wait for the man to ask, Barbara...'

She saw his face break into the familiar warm smile. 'That would be great,' he said, taking out his diary. 'That would be ... Sunday? The 4th?'

'Is that all right?'

'Yes, I look forward to it,' he said. 'Ah, here's our salad...'

Chapter Twelve

It was early on Friday evening and Constance Pargetter-Wilson was upstairs getting dressed. Her husband Geoffrey was spending the evening with his cronies at the golf club as he usually did while Constance prepared for her precious evening off, bathing leisurely and taking time over her clothes.

It was seven o clock when the telephone rang, and she cursed whoever it was. Wrapping herself in her housecoat, she picked up the phone in her bedroom. She wasn't best pleased to be called, whoever it was.

'Yes?'

It was her son, and she frowned to hear his voice.

'I can hardly hear you, dear, there's so much background noise. Where are you?'

'I'm at Heathrow, Mother, about to embark for Thailand.'

She'd forgotten he was going. Now what? she wondered.

'Are you all right? Nothing wrong?'

'No. Ma. My flight leaves in an hour, but I thought I'd let you know that I'm going on my own.'

'On your own? But I thought you said Joanna...'

'Yes, but she has to work, poor girl. Anyway, can't be helped. Just thought I'd give you a call.'

'Well, Dennis, take care.'

Silly boy, she thought, putting the phone down and tripping back to the bathroom where she took off her bathrobe and smoothed her legs, applying body lotion and afterwards eyeing them in the long mirror. Then from a small packet she withdrew a pair of silk stockings, her dark eyes gleaming with excitement.

She had seen them in Harrods when she last went to town and couldn't resist them. On the model leg on the counter they had looked bewitching: the front half plain black silk, the back intricately patterned silk openwork lace. Easing them on, she turned round to see the back view – wonderful – and fastened her narrow jewelled suspender belt on to the lacy tops, more than pleased that she had indulged herself and bought them. She wouldn't think about how much they had cost.

She sat down and peered at her flawless skin in the mirror, cleansed now and devoid of make-up, but couldn't resist a peep at her new lipstick. She put a dab on the back of her thumb – scarlet, real scarlet, not any old red – then slipped it in her handbag.

Snapping it closed, she stood up and finished dressing. A quarter of an hour later, she had locked up and was on her way to the garage. Thank goodness it was a fine night.

Dennis slipped the mobile into his pocket. Well, that was that. What the hell he was doing here on his own, he still couldn't imagine.

It had all happened the night before last, out of the blue. Joanna had joined him at a business conference in a super hotel out of town. The conference over, she had gone for some last-minute shopping while Dennis busied himself packing. Halfway through he had suddenly remembered a query to be put to his secretary, Diana. He had rung her, gone along to her room and sorted it out. He was just emerging when he saw Joanna get out of the lift, on her face what could only be described as a thunderous expression.

Back in their room, she tore into him. She shrieked, cried, thumped him, while he couldn't get a word in edgeways. After hours of being berated, slowly and painfully, he was forced to confess that he had taken the opportunity of Joanna's being out to have a quick snog with Diana. No amount of apologising was going to help. Joanna packed her bag and stormed out, crying, 'You bastard!' And as a last thrust, 'You know what you can do with your trip to Thailand.'

When the door closed behind her there was a strange silence. Dennis straightened his tie, took a deep breath, and checked through the window that his car was still in the car park. Thankfully she had taken a taxi or hired a car.

He sank on to the bed. He wouldn't have minded but he was practically innocent this time. He didn't even fancy Diana – she wasn't his type – not that he hadn't had a few other flings on the side, but Joanna wasn't to know that. He was only human after all. But to be accused of heaven knows what while innocent or as near as damn' it, that was the last straw. They had been due off to Thailand the day after tomorrow. Somehow he didn't think she'd be going.

Dennis never seemed to have much luck with women. Never had any difficulty finding one, it was holding on to them that was the problem.

He phoned Joanna twice the next day, but the office told him she was out of town.

Well, he was still going on holiday, he decided. He had already paid for it after all, and he wouldn't have minded but it had been Joanna's idea in the first place. Bloody hell. Serve her right if he had a fabulous time without her.

That would show her she couldn't push him around.

Simon and Susannah were lunching with her parents. It was a warm Sunday in early-May. The birds were singing, the tulips were out, and they were sitting in the garden having pre-lunch drinks. The scent from the wisteria on the house wall was intoxicating.

'How's business going?' Eric Whittaker asked. Always his first question.

'Very well – just secured another contract,' Simon said.

'Oh, where's that?'

'Maidenhead. We won't start until November.'

'Come into the study, I've something to

show you,' Eric said to him. 'I had a word with my brokers yesterday. You might be interested – your father too. No point in keeping something good to yourself, especially where close family is concerned.'

Simon smiled and dutifully followed his father-in-law inside the house.

Anne Whittaker stole a quick glance at Susannah. The girl looked pale – was she pregnant? Surely she would have told her mother? But something was obviously not right. There was no doubt she had sobered up since her marriage. One of the reasons, Anne felt sure, was that she didn't particularly like living at Fulford Manor. She missed her home, and Anne wondered if she was disappointed she hadn't started a baby yet.

'How is Aunt Felicity?' Susannah asked now.

'Oh, doing very nicely. It was bit of a shock – appendicitis seems to be somewhat old-fashioned these days, but anyway she was rushed to hospital and they dealt with it immediately. She says she feels fine, better than she has for ages.'

'I expect it had been coming on for some time,' Susannah said. 'Don't they call it a "rumbling appendix"?'

'I believe they do. Anyway, I've been trying to persuade her to come over for a visit. She's gone to Florida for a couple of weeks, but after that she says she'll think about it. I said we would spoil her and look after her – it would be lovely. After all, she didn't come for the wedding.'

For some reason Susannah felt a wave of depression at the news.

'Would she bring Jane?'

'Of course, darling, and Uncle Edwin if she likes. Anyway, we'll see what she says. It won't be until June or so. I'm looking forward to it already.'

Susannah had mixed feelings about this though she couldn't have said why. The thought of her cousin coming to England disquieted her.

She looked listless, Anne decided. Bored even. Surely she was happy with Simon? It had been all she had ever wanted – to marry him and start a family.

She decided to take the bull by the horns. After all, she was Susannah's mother.

She took a sip of her wine, and putting the glass back on the table, leaned forward to tuck a strand of her daughter's blonde hair behind her ear.

'Are you happy, darling?'

She saw Susannah start, as though she had been miles away.

'Happy?' She smiled, a wide false smile. 'Oh, Mummy, of course I am! How could you even ask?' Then she frowned. 'Well, I was hoping I might be pregnant by now.'

So that was it. Anne was relieved.

'Oh, darling, it does take time – you haven't been married that long.'

'Eleven months – almost a year. It will be our first wedding anniversary in June.'

'But you need a bit of time to yourselves,' Anne said. 'Once babies come along your life changes. For the better, of course,' she added hastily.

'Did you start a baby straight away?' Susannah looked so anxious Anne's heart bled for her.

'No,' she reassured her daughter. 'Your father was away quite a while, then when he came back...'

She didn't say that she had lost her first baby in a miscarriage at three and a half months for fear of worrying her daughter.

'And in any case,' she said, 'later on you can always have tests. Sometimes you can be over-anxious, and that doesn't help.'

She glanced at her watch.

'I think perhaps we should go in to lunch.

I expect it's ready by now.'

They went inside, and into Eric's study.

'Darling, it's almost one. I think it's time we went into the dining room.'

'So it is,' he said.

Simon went over to Susannah and put an arm round her shoulders.

'You feel warm from the sun,' he said, smiling down at her. 'Lead on, Macduff, I'm starving.'

They were driving home before Susannah mentioned the proposed visit of her aunt and her cousin to Simon, wondering why she had got herself so het up before doing so. After all, what difference should it make to him?

'I think Aunt Felicity may be coming over in June,' she said casually.

He kept his eyes on the road.

'I thought she'd been ill – appendicitis, wasn't it?'

'Yes, but she's better now. Recuperating in Florida.'

'Oh, that's nice,' he said. 'You missed her at the wedding, didn't you?'

'She wasn't well then.'

He doesn't ask if Jane will be coming, she thought.

'With your uncle?' he asked.

'I'm not sure,' she said. 'But with Jane, I expect,' knowing she was torturing herself – had built up her suspicions to a point where she was almost paranoid about it.

She couldn't look at him. Had he gone pale? Was he biting his cheek in the way he had if he was upset?

Suddenly he turned his head and gave her a swift warm smile, and she thrust her arm through his even though he was driving and snuggled up to him.

What on earth was the matter with her? Her nanny would have said she wanted her bottom smacked.

Barbara was sitting in the garden when her mobile phone rang. It was ten to eleven and she was drinking coffee. When she answered it was to hear the voice of Tim Riley from the bookshop.

'Barbara Cooper?' he asked.

'Yes.'

'Tim Riley,' he said. 'I was wondering if you were still interested in working in the bookshop?'

'Yes, I am,' she said, a surge of excitement rising.

'Would you be free to call in tomorrow, Wednesday, half-day, and perhaps we would talk about it then?'

'Oh, of course.'

'See you then. After lunch, about three?'

'About three,' Barbara said, switching off.

She had watched as the bookshop gradually filled up with new wooden shelves, and then the glass had been cleaned and a window display arranged. She could hardly stand and stare at it every day, but she was aware that it had opened the previous Monday.

Well, she would see. Not long to wait.

It looked quite different now, more commercial, she thought, for want of a better word. Not so much like an old-fashioned library. Tim was obviously a man of ideas. All the latest books were on show with large photographs of the authors, while the decor was comfortable, warm and enticing with its green walls and the occasional comfortable chair.

Different as it was from the old store, she felt at home at once.

There was a long counter with a computer and a cash till and opposite a desk with books casually displayed. She had to hand it to Tim – it was a great improvement.

He came towards her from the office and

held out his hand.

'I used to be a manager for W.H. Smith.'

'Oh!' And Barbara laughed.

'I won't tell you which branch, but I wanted to go out on my own.'

'Good for you,' she said.

'I know I'm taking a chance but you have to, don't you? Otherwise you'll never know what you're capable of. Do take a seat.'

Barbara sat down, feeling very much at ease.

'How long did you work here?' he asked.

'Five years. I used to work for the public library, but decided I was due for a change and this is very convenient.'

'Full-time, I suppose?'

'Yes, but I wouldn't want to do that now. I do a bit of charity work which I enjoy.'

He glanced down at her hand, seeing the wedding ring, and glanced away again.

'How would three days a week suit you?'

'Very well,' she said. 'Which days?'

'Tuesday, Thursday and Saturday, if that's convenient.'

'Every Saturday?'

'Three out of four. I'm hoping it will be a busy day.'

'It used to be the busiest,' she agreed.

'I'm hoping you can show me a thing or

two. I don't know the area.'

'Oh, I do wish you luck!' Barbara said impulsively.

'Thanks, I'm going to need all I can get,' he said. 'How do you rate my chances?'

'Well.' She hesitated. 'I think you've brought a new look to the shop, and that helps. My ex-boss was near to retirement age, and I have to say I think she rather let things slide so when the lease ran out, she was quite pleased to go.'

Barbara looked around. 'But this is exciting,' she said approvingly. 'I love the decor, I'm sure it will make people feel they want to come in, and they will be drawn by the window display. I know I was.'

He looked pleased. 'Now about hours ... and when could you start?'

'Next week,' she said. 'That will give me the weekend to put my affairs in order.'

'Do you have children?'

'Oh, no,' she said. 'I'm a widow.' As if that made any difference, and found herself blushing as she had once before.

'Well, Barbara,' he said. 'Nine-thirty till five, OK? Saturday we'll leave open. How did you find Saturdays – were the mornings the busiest?'

'Yes, that's true.'

'And about money...' He went off into further discussion on hours and payment, and Barbara left the shop convinced she was doing the right thing. Everything was working out well. It would leave her Wednesdays free to work in the charity shop and the odd days for shopping and housework. She almost hummed as she made her way towards the other shops.

When the postman came before Ben left for school, he always picked up the letters lying on the mat. It was a special treat. But he rarely found one for himself except for birthdays. But he was lucky today and he knew who it was from – his father. His address in Florida was written on the back – only Americans did that. But the front – ah, the front was addressed to Ben McKay, Sunnyside, Birch Common, Bucks, England.

He ran with it to his mother in the kitchen, his face flushed with excitement, his eyes shining. She took it from him, then handed it back.

'Well, open it.'

He did so carefully. The note was written on a postcard of a dolphin and was quite short.

LOOK FORWARD TO SEEING YOU IN JUNE. LOVE DADDY. LETTER FOLLOWING.

'He's coming home – he's coming home in June!' Ben shouted, jumping up and down.

His mother read the note and stared out of the window.

Typical, she thought. Absolutely typical. Not a word to me. No, May I? Is it convenient?

Ben threw his arms round her and held her tight. She looked down at the mop of hair so like his father's, and bent to kiss him.

'Yes, that's super,' she said. 'Absolutely super.'

Now get out of that one, Viv McKay, she told herself.

Constance had been to an afternoon council meeting, had aired her views in a thoroughly forceful manner, as was her wont, and was satisfied with her performance.

She had been agitating for years for the old Victorian house called Charlton Manor on the road between Texbury and Birch Common to be turned into a nursing home for the aged. It had eight bedrooms and was badly in need of renovation. Empty since the last occupant had died, the council had reluctantly taken it over. Now they were aware that its current market price had leapt astonishingly in the three years they had owned it and had decided to debate its future use.

Battles had been fought by various members but, as usual, Constance had won the day by appealing to their better natures. Some of them could see vast profits if their own ideas for development went ahead, but Constance and her nursing home had triumphed.

She got into her car and drove home, fully satisfied, glancing briefly at Charlton House as she passed it, sitting forlornly in its overgrown garden, both its iron gates broken and leaning drunkenly to one side.

Oh yes, she could visualise it all. She mentally repaired the gates, cleared the drive, and had all the oldies sitting out on the immaculate lawn taking tea when their loving relatives came to visit them.

Once home she checked her housekeeper had left the meal prepared. Constance just had to put it in the oven for forty minutes – chicken casserole, her favourite – put on the potatoes, and last of all the frozen broccoli.

She hummed to herself as she took off her

black suit, and went into the bathroom. She and Geoffrey would have a quiet night in, possibly watch television, not that either of them was bothered about it. Still, she enjoyed these evenings when she and her husband would discuss their busy days and the progress they had made.

She was halfway through soaping her arms when for some unknown reason she thought of Dennis – and froze.

Had he not been gone rather a long time? They had had a couple of e-mails from him the first week or so but nothing since. Now when did he go? April it must have been – and now it was early-May. She had to admit to herself that she was a little worried. In the Far East all sorts of things happened – but mostly to girls, she reassured herself. Anyway, Dennis was a grown man and well able to look after himself.

She stepped out of the bath and dried herself, putting her watch back on and glancing at the time. Five-forty – too late to ring Dennis's office. Anyway, Geoffrey would be home soon. Changing into a flowery housecoat, which she usually did for evenings in, she made her way downstairs to check the oven.

She was waiting for her husband with a

drink already poured when he came in, and thought as she sometimes did what a handsome man he still was. He had managed to keep his figure fairly well, golf and regular exercise took care of that, and she knew quite a few women envied her.

He was also slightly out of breath.

'Everything all right, Geoffrey?' she asked.

'Had a phone call just as I was leaving the office.'

'Phone call? Who was it?'

'Dennis. He said he'd tried to call you but couldn't seem to get through. I told him you were at a council meeting.'

'Is he all right? Where is he?'

'His plane was diverted to Paris or so he says and he was getting the next flight out. So he'll be here any minute.'

Geoffrey glanced up at the clock.

'He's coming straight over?'

Well, of course she was anxious to see her son. Still, it did put a stop to their quiet evening in together.

'I'll just go upstairs and change. Be down again in a minute,' her husband said.

She thumbed through a magazine. Funny she should have thought about Dennis only this afternoon. Telepathy, I shouldn't wonder, she decided.

Just as Geoffrey re-entered the room, the phone rang.

'Hello? Oh, Dennis,' she said. 'How are you, dear? Yes ... where? Heathrow, right ... expect you within the hour then.'

She put down the phone and sighed.

'He's on his way,' she said. 'I must say, it seems an age since he went.'

'Almost a month,' Geoffrey said.

'I thought that this afternoon. Lord, I hope we can make the casserole stretch, he's sure to be hungry.'

'We could go out,' Geoffrey suggested. 'Go over to The Bear.'

'No, we'll stay in. He's bound to want to talk about his trip.'

'Fine. Now how did you get on with the council?' He picked up his whisky.

'Wonderfully! Well, I won the argument, didn't I?' She purred like a cat who'd got the cream.

'And they were quite happy with it?'

'Well, I don't know about that, but they voted it in and now it will go before the planning committee.'

'Well done,' he said.

'I'll just go into the dining room and lay another place,' she said, returning after a few moments.

'Top up?' he asked.

'Yes, please, dear.'

It seemed no time before they heard the taxi drive up and stop at the front entrance.

'Ah, there he is,' Constance said, finding she was quite pleased at the thought of seeing her son again. It had been a long time after all.

The key turned in the lock, and she heard voices – the taxi driver being paid off. Then Dennis's voice.

'This way.'

The door of the drawing room was pushed open and Dennis, a big grin on his sun-tanned face, came in ushering in a tiny Chinese girl before him. She was half his height, with narrow black eyes and shiny black hair worn in a fringe. She was casually dressed in black jeans and a white sweater. Inconsequentially Constance thought, she must be a size six at most. She didn't look nervous at all to find herself in a strange place, her black eyes danced merrily.

'Mother, Dad, I'd like you to meet Mai Ling – we're going to be married.'

Chapter Thirteen

Constance's first thought was, and here I am in my housecoat, meeting my future daughter-in-law. But there was nothing she could do about it now. Finding her voice, she went over and took Mai Ling's hand. She positively sailed the few steps to reach the girl.

'How do you do?' Then it was Geoffrey's turn to greet her. He did so, looking by turns uncomfortable and unable to hide his astonishment.

'My dear,' he said.

Looking down at this diminutive girl with her sparkling black eyes he somehow felt that Dennis might at last have met his match. There was humour there, and a quiet determination in the small firm chin.

Dennis, having got that over, breathed a sigh of relief. 'Let's go in and sit down, shall we? I think drinks are called for – no, not champagne, Father, we'll save that for later.'

'Of course,' Geoffrey said, going over to the cabinet. 'A nice Beaujolais or perhaps some white? I think we have chicken for dinner.'

Dennis seems very sure of himself, Constance thought.

'If you'll excuse me,' she said, more to steady herself than anything, 'I'll just nip upstairs and put on something more suitable before I go into the kitchen and see how the dinner is going. We weren't expecting visitors,' she confided with one of her most winning smiles. What ever had happened to her maxim that you should never excuse yourself before visitors?

'I thought we'd go out,' Dennis said.

'Would you like to?' his father enquired.

But Constance needed time to get used to this situation.

'No, I'm sure we can manage. A few extra vegetables ... it's already in the oven.'

She disappeared upstairs and came down in a few moments wearing her usual black skirt and white blouse.

'I'm just off to the kitchen,' she said. 'I won't be a moment.'

'I will help,' said Mai Ling, following her much to Constance's dismay. She tripped behind her hostess, her tiny feet making no sound.

'Have you lettuce?' she asked. 'I will see to

241

the salad.' She went straight over to the fridge and to Constance's horror took out a lettuce from the dewbin. 'Some tomatoes–' she called them tomaytoes '–ah, and a green pepper.'

'You really mustn't...' Constance began, not sure as to whether she should be pleased with this offer of help or shocked by the situation. No one ever entered her kitchen but Constance herself and her housekeeper.

Mai Ling took down the chopping board. She sought out a sharp knife and began chopping it all expertly, looking round for a salad bowl which Constance found herself mutely taking out from the china cupboard and handing over. She found the salad servers too and then opened the oven door to see the chicken casserole bubbling steadily.

'Have you 'erbs?' Mai Ling asked.

'What? Oh, herbs,' Constance said. 'Yes, of course.'

Mai Ling peered inside the oven too. 'Ah, that's lovely,' she said. 'Plenty for four.'

'Excuse me.' Constance had never felt so useless in her life, she who was used to taking charge. 'I must go and lay another place.'

This she did, adding more glasses and

extra cutlery, and came back to find Mai Ling walking towards her carrying a large bowl of salad.

'Put it there, dear,' she said, and felt it was time she took over. 'There's plenty of time, the dinner can wait. You go on into the drawing room, I've put everything on low.'

Mai Ling gracefully concurred and they were soon joined there by Constance who had recovered now and was determined to take her rightful place as hostess once more.

By now they all had drinks. After taking a sip of hers, Constance put her glass down on the table.

'Now,' she said pleasantly, 'tell us all about it. Where did you meet – and how? We want to hear everything.' And she beamed across at Geoffrey who, taking his cue from her, smiled broadly back. He knew he could safely leave this to his wife.

Dennis took one of his fiancée's hands in his.

'Mai is a practising doctor, she lives in London and works at St Thomas's Hospital.'

Shock number one, thought Constance, but at least she lives in London.

'How did you meet?' she asked, being careful to beam one of her confidence-inspiring smiles.

'At a night club. Mai was on holiday too and, well,' he smiled at her, 'we just clicked.'

And a more oddly assorted pair I can't imagine, thought Constance. Still, if she is the one who will give Dennis stability, and if he really loves her...

There seemed to be no doubt about that. But Dr Ling is firmly in charge, thought Constance. And I must say that could be a blessed relief – if things work out all right. Knee-high to a grasshopper, nevertheless she seems more capable than a woman twice her size.

Mai Ling's bright black eyes darted from one of her prospective parents-in-law to the other. Her exquisite small hands bore no rings as yet, but when she looked at Dennis it was as if he was the love of her life.

Oh, I do hope so, prayed Constance. I don't mind if she's an Eskimo as long as they settle down and she makes him happy. He respects her, she thought, and that's a good start. She wondered what Geoffrey was thinking.

'Well, have you made any plans?'

The young couple looked at each other.

'Yes, a small wedding, we thought, in July perhaps. Mai Ling's parents are in Hong Kong, and we shall be going there for the ceremony. So, Mother, as soon as we've fixed the date, I'll let you and Dad know. A trip to Hong Kong would be great, wouldn't it?'

A wedding! Constance thought. Well, that sounded definite enough. Not just living together, then. Will Mai keep her own name after the wedding? Somehow Doctor Pargetter-Wilson didn't sound quite right.

Well, she thought as she went into the kitchen closely followed by Mai Ling, to put extra frozen broccoli into the boiling water, this day had started off like any other. Who would have thought it?

Later that evening when Geoffrey joined her in their room with its twin beds neatly ranged side by side, he stood in his striped pyjamas, winding the bedside clock and opened his mouth. 'Er...'

Constance held up a restraining hand. 'Leave it 'til the morning, Geoffrey. Goodnight, dear.'

'Sleep well,' he said. But both of them lay awake long after the light was switched off.

Barbara was preparing lunch. The kitchen window stood open wide, the sun shone on the small lawn and the apple tree. Late tulips and wallflowers scented the garden, and she had put chairs out beneath the umbrella which she would raise if the sun became too bright.

She was expecting Georgie Taylor from the Indian trip. Her friend was motoring down from London, and Barbara was really looking forward to seeing her again.

She had prepared Vichyssoise, followed by cold salmon and salad, with strawberries and cream to follow.

After a last-minute look around the house, the dining table laid, the flowers fresh in the small sitting room, she picked up the Sunday papers.

Just after twelve the sound of Georgie's car coming to a stop outside her front door alerted her. You could always park outside your own residence on Birch Common, and there Georgie was, locking her car, looking so familiar in a black trouser suit, her dark hair closely cut, carrying a Prada handbag.

Barbara smiled to herself. So nice that she could come, yet strange to see her out of context. She went to the front door.

'Georgie! Lovely to see you. You found it all right then?'

'No problem, straight down the A40, your directions were perfect. I say, this is nice and cosy.'

'Come on in,' Barbara said. 'Do you want to take off your jacket?'

'No, I'll stay as I am at the moment. Golly, this is nice,' as Barbara led her through the hall into the sitting room. 'You can't imagine how good it is to get out of London on a Sunday and come a-visiting to leafy Bucks.'

'Sit down,' Barbara said. 'I thought we'd have a drink outside – it's such a nice day. Lunch at 1.15 – is that all right?'

'Super,' Georgie said, seating herself in an easy chair. 'I tried to visualise your little house, but it's completely different from what I imagined. More...'

'Twee?' suggested Barbara.

Georgie laughed. 'No, I didn't mean that at all. It's all so comfortable, with such lovely things. I haven't anything like this. My flat is very basic.'

'Mostly inherited from my in-laws,' Barbara confessed. 'But it suits me – at least for the time being. Now what would you like? Red wine ... whatever. I've most things, I think.'

'Wine would be nice,' Georgie said, looking around. 'This is you on your wedding day, I suppose?' looking at a photograph on a side table.

'Yes,' Barbara said, going to the sideboard and pouring drinks. 'Long time ago now.'

'He looks nice, your William.'

'He was, and I still miss him. Shall we take them outside?'

'Yes, sure. Oh, what a pretty garden. Do you do it?'

'Yes. I used not to, William did. I cope now, but I'm quite enjoying it. His parents kept it so beautifully while all I can manage to do is keep it in check. Still, it's good for me.'

When they had settled, Georgie looked across at her and smiled. 'And what are you up to?'

Barbara pushed the bowl of olives and nuts towards her.

'Got a job,' she said triumphantly.

'No!'

'In the old bookshop where I used to work – it's under new ownership. An ex-manager from W.H. Smith.'

'Should know what he's doing then,' Georgie said, helping herself to olives. 'What about your charity work?'

'Still do half a day – I enjoy it. But tell me what you've been up to?'

'You won't believe me when I tell you.'

'You've changed your job?' Barbara guessed.

'I wish. No, nothing like that. But I have been seeing James.'

'Not James...'

'James Stevens, the doctor, the one on the Indian trip.'

Barbara sat open-mouthed.

'No! I thought he lived in Bath?'

Georgie grinned. 'Well, he does, that's where his practice is – but he comes up from time to time.'

'Oh, but that's wonderful. Are you – er – an item as they say?'

'Could be.' Georgie sipped her wine. 'I've grown really fond of him, Barbara. I suppose you think we're very different and what would I be doing with a man like that?'

'No,' Barbara said seriously. 'I'm delighted for you, especially if you like each other.'

'Well, we've sort of grown together. I have to admit, he's not my usual type but there's something about him...'

'I liked him,' Barbara said.

'Did you? I'm glad. Because,' Georgie said slowly, 'I think we are going to be married – eventually. Well, I hope so. At the moment he's in the process of selling his house in Batheaston and applying for a job in a London hospital.'

'Well!' Barbara said. 'That *is* good news.'

During lunch they talked about the Indian trip and the people they'd met on it, laughing hilariously at certain memories.

'So what about Bryan?' Georgie asked, and saw Barbara flush.

'Bryan? Oh, well, we've had lunch together a few times – he's awfully nice. A widower,' she added unnecessarily.

'I know,' Georgie said. 'And?'

'He came down to lunch a couple of weeks ago...'

'And how was it?'

Barbara raised her eyebrows.

'Well, you know, sometimes when you see people in their own environment it's different – like us – yet you seem to fit in here so well,' Georgie said.

Barbara thought about it. 'Well, he did too. He looked very at home. Sat in William's chair which gave me an odd feeling.'

'But did you mind?'

'No,' Barbara said hastily. 'Of course not.'

'You'd make a nice couple,' her friend encouraged her.

'I have to say, I'm very attracted to him, Georgie. The first man I've really been interested in since William died.'

'Well, that's wonderful, and I'm sure he feels the same way about you.

'Yes, I think he does. He hasn't actually said anything but...'

'He will,' Georgie said firmly. 'He's building up to it – and then what will you say?'

'I'm tempted but not sure. I can't quite imagine what our lifestyle would be, and that's important to me.'

'Oh, well, if you're going to let a little thing like that stand in the way!' Georgie laughed, and Barbara laughed with her.

After the strawberries Barbara made coffee to take outside. She put up the sun umbrella. The light was quite bright, and it was peaceful and quiet under the apple tree now full of blossom.

'I wanted to see you today,' Georgie began, 'because you make good listener and I've something to tell you.'

'Oh? I thought you already had.'

'No, seriously. Did I tell you James had been married?'

'No, I don't think I knew that.'

'Well, his wife left him. He's been quite honest about it with me. There was an incident at the surgery where he works – an elderly patient died – and the family complained James hadn't done enough, hadn't realised how ill she was.'

'Oh, how awful!'

'Well, while all this was going on, because the family sued, James's wife left him. Said she couldn't stomach a problem like that, doubts about his ability and so on, and walked out.'

'What a thing to do! Just when he needed her support.'

'Exactly. So that was that. Of course, there was nothing to it, there were profuse apologies all round – but James said it's left its mark. It's an awful thing to experience.'

'I can imagine. No wonder he looked fed up when he arrived on the trip.'

'Yes, it was his first break after the case. Anyway he emerged without a stain on his character. He's a very good man, Barbara, and he's been really hurt by this.'

'And you've obviously grown very fond of him,' she said. 'You're not confusing love with sympathy?'

'No. I've thought hard about it, and I feel as I've never felt about a man before. I've had several men friends, Barbara. Sounds like *Jesus Christ Superstar*, doesn't it? So many men, in so many ways. Seriously, this is different, I'm sure we could make a go of it. That's why I wanted to see you – because you've met him.'

'Good for you!' Barbara said. She was all

for a bit of romance.

'So tell me what life is like in this little oasis? Do you know many neighbours? Have you friends locally?'

'I've got to know more people since William died and I've been at home – one woman, in particular, I've become close friends with. Viv – you met her briefly at the airport.'

'Oh, yes. How is she?'

And Barbara told her.

Viv sent George an e-mail.

Rather short notice, isn't it? I had planned to take a few days off in June – thought I might take a trip. All well here.
Viv.

He replied:

So much the better – I thought Ben would be at school. Expect me around the 28th. I'll confirm later. Love, George.

Going back to the common room he sank into a leather chair next to his campus friend. Mark came from Bristol and they had struck up a friendship early on.

'Well, that's done,' George sighed.

They were silent for a few minutes.

'My year will be up soon,' he said. 'I've a choice of staying for a further year or applying for Kingston Ontario. Maybe something else at home, too – I'm waiting to hear.'

'You know, I've been thinking,' Mark said. 'On reflection, I don't think you handled this move to the States all that well.'

'And you'd know,' George commented. 'After your two divorces.'

'OK, so I'm no expert. But I have learned a lot about women.'

'Sounds as if you've had plenty of experience,' George said drily.

'You can jeer all you like, but from where I'm sitting, I think you were pretty heavy-handed.'

'What?'

'Well, from what I gather, you didn't ask Viv to come.'

'You mean, get her permission?'

'No, I mean you just assumed she would pack and follow. That's always a mistake. Women like to be asked.'

'But we're talking about our whole life together – our joint future, my role as husband and father.'

'OK. But did you talk it over with her

beforehand – ask her what she thought about the job application?'

George looked astonished.

'I don't get you. I naturally assumed she would come if I got it.'

'Automatically?'

'Well, yes.'

'Ah, well, in my opinion, George, I think that's where you went wrong. Women like to be deferred to – or at least consulted. After all, you've got the excitement and satisfaction of a new job while she's just expected to trail behind.'

'Oh, come on, she's my wife!'

'But not your chattel,' Mark said.

There was a long silence.

'Anyway, someone else is consoling her now,' Mark said.

'Didn't waste much time, did she?' George sounded bitter.

'Well, it is almost a year,' Mark said, and stood up, stretching himself.

'I'm for bed. Goodnight, George.'

He sat on for a long time in his easy chair.

He missed Viv as much as he missed his son. There was job satisfaction here, no doubt about that, but what really mattered most to him? He liked the States, personally, although he preferred the UK, but the opportunities here were so good. The money was better than at home too. He had almost decided against Kingston, but another year here... Viv wouldn't put up with it and that would signal the end of the marriage. In all truth, he had overlooked her job. She was up for promotion – of course it was important to her, as important as his job was to him.

He felt quite noble at the end of this self-assessment. Anyway he missed her beside him in the big double bed. As for Ben, he had already missed a year out of his son's childhood. Viv was a fantastic mother, he freely admitted, as well as a good wife and an exciting lover. No one could take her place. She was strong and courageous, too. Look how she had stood up to him. It had been a regular battle of wills – one he could see now he had been determined to win.

Of course there were pretty girls on the campus, plenty of them, but they weren't like Viv. She knew her attractions better than anyone – knew she could draw men. Look at the message in his mother-in-law's card. At the thought of someone else sleeping with Viv, his gorge rose. And yet women were free to do those things today, especially when deserted by their husbands.

He thought of his own parents, loving and tender with each other, like a pair of lovebirds. His mother would never have allowed his father to go off on his own – she would have been right there behind him. But today things were different as Viv had rightly pointed out to him. He had a sudden longing for her. The way when he put his hand tenderly on her body she would turn to him, warm and generous, ever ready for his lovemaking – how could he have given that up?

His mind was made up by the time he went to bed. In the morning he would send a message to say he was coming home, and when he was back with Viv and Ben he'd tell them it would soon be for good.

Viv and Ben went to Heathrow to meet George's plane. Ben had been in such a state of excitement he could barely contain himself. When George appeared from Customs he let go of Viv's hand and ran to throw himself at his father.

'Hey! Hey!' George said, grinning all over his face. 'You've grown!' he said, putting the boy down and kissing Viv lightly on the cheek. They loaded a trolley, and with his arm lightly across her shoulders walked out towards the car park.

Once home, she put the kettle on.

'Peter couldn't come today – he's refereeing a football match,' Ben said.

'Who's Peter?' George asked, glancing at Viv who seemed too busy making the tea to catch his eye.

'A friend of ours,' Ben said. 'Sometimes he takes me to play football. He used to be in the Arsenal reserves.'

'Oh,' George said, but there was such a clatter of cups and saucers and tea plates he could hardly hear himself speak.

Later he bathed Ben, which seemed to take forever, and read him a story, then went downstairs where Viv had poured them drinks. They both seemed strangely subdued.

George broke the silence first.

'I'm coming home in July,' he said abruptly.

Viv stared at him.

'For good?' she asked him suspiciously.

'Yes. I've handed in my notice.' He saw her eyes brim over.

'Oh, George!' She flung herself at him and he gathered her into his arms and covered her face in kisses. They stood like that for a long time, just holding each other.

Presently they went upstairs together, arms around each other, and Ben quickly hopped into his bed because he had been on the floor with his Lego. He pulled the sheet up over his eyes in case they came in.

But he needn't have worried. They went on into their own room, and he was soon asleep because they didn't seem to be talking or arguing. In fact, he thought he heard someone laugh once.

Chapter Fourteen

It was the last day of June and Anne Whittaker and her sister Felicity, together with Jane, had just arrived back from London, armed with boxes and packages from their shopping expedition to Knightsbridge.

Eric and his brother-in-law Edwin sat in the garden of Kirby Lodge, drinking champagne to celebrate Felicity's return to health and the fact that they were all together at last.

'Yes, I needed the break. It's some years since I came over but I'm pleased to see everything looks the same. The house and garden that is ... been a bit of a year all round, eh, Eric?'

'It certainly has,' he agreed, and Edwin knew he was referring to Felicity's illness and the death of Jane's fiancé Richard.

'Quite a year,' he repeated.

'Looking forward to Scotland?' Eric asked.

'Yes. It's a pity Jane doesn't want to come

with us. Still, I expect she'll be happier with the young folks,' Edwin said.

'We shall be going over to the Rawnsleys' for lunch tomorrow,' Eric said. 'You'll be interested in the set up there, Edwin. Quite incredible the way Her Ladyship – Simon's mother – has turned the tables although I have to admit she works very hard at it. I imagine you have to make a tourist attraction out of a place like that if you want to make money. After all, it's hardly a major stately home. Still, it has its interest, and she leaves no stone unturned to find new ways and means of bringing in the tourists.'

'And Susannah – is she settling down in her new life?'

'Oh, yes, I think so. We don't see so much of Simon, although she often comes over on her own for lunch during the week. We're always pleased to see her, of course.'

'I imagine so,' Edwin said. 'Comes of having all your eggs in one basket, Eric.'

'True,' he said.

An hour later, bathed and changed, the ladies made their way down the steps to the lawn.

'Ah, here they are.' Eric stood up as Anne, Felicity and Jane emerged from the house.

Jane bent down and kissed her father.

'Hallo, Daddy,' she said, her brown eyes lighting up at the sight of him.

'I hope you haven't broken the bank.'

'I think we have,' Felicity confessed. 'We tried anyway. Still, we're not over here very often.'

'How about a drink?' Eric asked, eyeing the champagne cooling in the ice bucket.

'Why not?' Felicity said.

'Not for me,' Jane said. 'I think I'll take a walk around the paddock.'

'No horses now, dear,' Anne said ruefully. 'They're over with Simon and Susannah. It's a funny thing but I miss them – although Eric and I don't ride.'

'Yes, I can't imagine being without horses, although we don't have them in New York, of course. We always seem to be in Virginia these days, thanks to Jane. She'd live there if she could,' sighed Felicity.

They watched her neat figure retreating as she made her way across the lawns to the fence enclosing the paddock.

'It was a terrible thing, Richard's dying like that,' Eric said. 'And the timing too – just before her cousin's wedding.'

'Yes, he was so young, the whole world in front of him. Everything you'd want in a son-in-law ... rich, handsome. It'll take her a while to get over it.'

'It's worrying for you, Flick. Let's hope she meets someone else. Well, she's bound to with those looks.'

'Yes, she is attractive, but she goes round like a zombie. I was surprised she agreed to come over with us, and even then she only made up her mind at the last minute. As I say, she spends very little time in New York. We're just playing it by ear, as the saying goes.'

Jane walked round the empty stables, cleared now of horses and swept clean, some harnesses still hanging on the great wooden pegs, the walls lined with the various accoutrements of riding. A lump came in her throat. Stupid to stand here expecting Simon to come to her aid as he had once before.

She kicked at the turf and flopped down on a stool, legs stretched out in front of her, eyes staring vacantly into space. She wondered what her parents would think if they knew her real reason for accompanying them. She wanted above anything else to see Simon again.

No matter that he had been recently married her cousin Susannah, the emotions he had aroused in her, and the way he had said he felt about her, had been irresistible. She had never felt that with Richard. She had loved him, known he was a good man, her parents had approved of him and he was rich. All those things mattered to her, but not as much as the one really important thing: how she'd felt about him. And it was nothing like her feelings for Simon, who had brought her alive. It was if she had never really lived or been conscious of anything going on around her before she met him. She dreamed night after night of his arms about her, the way he had looked and held her. She had fled back to New York, in fear and trembling, afraid of what she might do if she stayed.

She had been mad to come back here, had known it before she had agreed to accompany her parents. It was just adding further misery. What could it possibly achieve? It only compounded her misery to know that he was going through the same turmoil.

She knew now there would be no one else who would matter to her as much as he did. She was sure of that. Susannah and Simon did not belong together. Jane had convinced herself that Susannah had never really loved him, not in the way she did. They were more like brother and sister. She had persuaded herself of this as the days wore on, and her mother waited for her to decide whether or not she would accompany them to London.

In the end, it was too much. She had to give in. She could no more pass up an opportunity to see Simon again than fly in the air. She hadn't given much thought to what would happen when they did meet, if he still felt the same – she just had to see him again.

Now her heart began to thud as she thought of the journey to the Rawnsleys' house tomorrow. Simon in his own setting – she could hardly wait. But she must keep cool and never give her parents the slightest idea of what she was feeling. They would be horrified to know she had an ulterior motive. No, those words were too harsh. She just wanted to see him again.

The five of them set off in time to arrive for lunch, her parents commenting along the way on the beauties of the English countryside in summer, the pretty villages along the Thames Valley, while Jane saw nothing, or very little, so immersed was she in the thought of seeing Simon again.

On the outskirts of Henley, when the car turned in at the wide iron gates of Fulford

Manor, she stifled a gasp. It was breath-taking. The view of the house from the entrance was every bit as imposing as any of Britain's stately homes.

'My word!' breathed Felicity, while Edwin sat open-mouthed.

'I had no idea it was as grand as this,' he said eventually.

'Imagine what it takes to keep up,' Eric said as they drove up the long approach. 'But they are the nicest couple, aren't they, Anne?'

It was rather splendid, Anne thought, and glancing at Jane who had said nothing was surprised at the look in those great dark eyes. They held a gleam almost of antici-pation. Natural enough, perhaps, but she wondered as she had before why she sometimes felt there was something a little disconcerting about her attractive niece.

But all worrying thoughts were put aside as Simon and Susannah, together with his parents, appeared at the top of the steps, waiting to greet their guests.

There were joyful hugs and kisses and introductions all round. Anne, alert after her own observations in the car, was not slow to recognise the slight look of appre-hension on Susannah's face as she leaned forward to kiss her cousin.

Simon held out his hand and kissed all three ladies once on each cheek while Susannah hugged her father.

'Now shall we go into the house?' asked Lady Rawnsley, putting an arm through each girl's and leading them inside.

Neither Simon nor Jane had met each other's eyes.

Once inside the house, the newcomers looked around appreciatively, commenting on the great fireplace, now filled with flowers, the double staircase, when all Jane wanted to do was to look at Simon.

He was just the same as she remembered, every feature of his face: the blue eyes, the slicked back golden hair, the firmness of his chin. She could have been transported straight back to her previous visit. Simon didn't even glance her way which was odd, she thought. As host to an attractive young woman and her parents he surely should acknowledge her. He was afraid to meet her eyes, she told herself, and a fierce pang of jealousy ran through her as she watched Susannah slide her arm through his. He's mine, she seemed to say.

Jane glanced at her cousin, still as pretty as ever, her blonde hair tied back, her face fresh as an English rose – but her eyes betrayed her, Jane thought. That instinctive awareness of the significance of other people's expressions might have surprised her mother who had yet to realise that her beloved daughter was more observant than she often appeared.

There were faint blue smudges under Susannah's eyes which denoted lack of sleep – and not for the obvious reason, Jane thought, aware that she had chosen to put a construction on Susannah's appearance to suit herself. She hadn't wanted to find her cousin relaxed and carefree and happy. She also accepted that her present situation brought out the very worst in her own character, but there was nothing she could do about it now.

'We'll go through to the garden for pre-lunch drinks,' Lady Rawnsley said, 'and later on you might like to look over the house. It has many features you might find interesting.'

The view from the back terrace was breathtaking, and when they had settled themselves Lord Rawnsley asked them what they would like to drink.

'I'm taking orders,' he said. 'My job on a Sunday when our so-called butler has his day off. He lives with his family in the village, and we call on him only when we must. Visitors from overseas, that sort of thing.'

'Well, we'll excuse your butlerless situation,' Edwin chuckled, 'although I have to say I would have liked to have been waited on by a real old English butler.'

Lord Rawnsley smiled. 'Old being the operative word,' he said. 'He's a grandfather, been here since my father's time. Otherwise, we have an excellent housekeeper who even now is cooking lunch for us.' He smiled at his wife. 'Joan here is the one who keeps it all going. Without her I can't imagine how we would manage.'

'Well, you're not going to be without me,' Lady Joan said firmly. 'Felicity, what will you have?'

Jane glanced across at the view of parkland stretching into the distance. All this, and Simon too.

'I'll help you, Dad,' he said, getting up to follow Lord Rawnsley into the house.

Susannah leaned back in her chair, feeling slightly more relaxed. The fears she had unaccountably nursed about her cousin seemed ridiculous now. Simon had barely acknowledged Jane. She had let her own

uncertainties run wild until they had fest-
ered. Whatever the troubles were between
herself and Simon, she could hardly blame
Jane for them.

She looked across at her cousin. Jane sat
staring into space, her lovely dark eyes
almost glittering. Determined to be friendly
to this girl who seemed so aloof, Susannah
smiled her.

'It's beautiful here, isn't it, Jane? And so
lovely to be sitting out on a sunny day –
we've had so much rain this year, we
thought it would never end.'

'Where is your house?' Jane asked.

'You can't see it from here, it's behind the
oak trees. There, you can just catch a
glimpse of it. We'll go over and see it later, if
you like.'

'Of course,' Felicity said, 'you will move
into the Manor when...'

'Oh, not for a long time yet. I'm perfectly
happy where we are for the moment.
Anyway, moving here means I'd have to take
over the tourist side of things and Joan is so
good at it.'

'I'm sure you would manage perfectly,'
Felicity said. 'Ah, here come the men.'

They set down two trays of drinks on the
table.

'G and T for Aunt Felicity. White wine for Jane and Susannah.'

'Thank you.'

Conversation flowed around the table until Lady Rawnsley asked Jane directly in which part of Virginia their home was.

'We have a ranch at Blue Cedars about twenty miles from Richmond,' she answered.

'I understand you spend almost all your time there?'

Jane smiled. 'Well, Mummy says I'm horse mad, and I suppose I am.'

'How many do you keep?'

'Fourteen at the last count.'

'Oh, my goodness! You must see if you can fit in a ride while you are here. Susannah brought over her three when she came to live at the Dower House. My husband and I used to ride a lot, but seldom manage it these days except for the hunt.'

Once during lunch Jane thought she felt Simon's eyes on her, but when she looked up he quickly lowered them.

It was an uneventful interlude, a typically English meal served in the beautifully appointed dining room, with the conversation light and inconsequential. Jane sometimes joined in, but only usually when she was asked a direct question. Several times Felicity caught her husband's eye, knowing he too had perceived Jane's off-handedness. Perhaps she wished she hadn't come. She was so difficult these days, a fact they blamed on the loss of her fiancé.

They moved outside to the terrace for coffee. Lady Joan seemed to take pity on Jane, and moved her chair to sit beside her.

'Now tell me what you have been doing since you arrived. I know you went shopping yesterday – what do you think of our shops?'

'Wonderful,' Jane said, grateful for the effort that was being made. 'I love our shops in New York but sometimes in London you can find cute little places that are really interesting, where they sell odd things you would never find at home, and I love the markets.'

'Oh, I'm glad you're enjoying it. Are you going to spend some time here with Simon and Susannah? I understand you weren't that keen to go to Scotland.'

Jane felt the blood rush to her cheeks.

'I'm not sure what the plan is,' she said hastily.

'When we've finished our coffee you'll enjoy going over to see their little house. It's very sweet, and Susannah has made it so comfortable.'

It was indeed difficult to talk to this very attractive American girl, thought Joan. Even now she might be in the same position as Susannah as a new young wife if tragedy had not overtaken her.

'Take your time,' she said, getting up. 'I'm just going to have a word with your mother. I expect your parents will want to come back inside the house and look over it.'

Presently Susannah and Simon stood up and came over to Jane who felt her heart begin to beat rapidly.

'Jane, we're going to make our way over to the Dower House. Would you like to see it?'

She stood up. 'Yes, I'd love to,' she said, putting her cardigan around her shoulders.

'Have you been keeping well?' he asked.

'Living at the stables, according to your mother,' Susannah laughed.

Jane ignored her and turned to Simon. 'As a matter of fact, I'm thinking of starting a riding school.'

'Good idea,' he said.

'Quite ambitious,' Susannah commented.

They had followed the path round and now the Dower House came into view. It really was the prettiest place, set among

273

greenery and covered with ivy, with a deep pink rose clambering over the front door.

'It's beautiful,' Jane said involuntarily.

Susannah took Simon's hand and looked up at him. 'We think so, don't we, darling?'

Before they reached the house Jane wondered what on earth she was doing here, chasing a dream, torturing herself with thoughts of what might have been. Her envy was so strong she could hardly bear it.

Simon turned the key in the front door and smiled down at her.

'There,' he said. 'Welcome to the Dower House.'

It was all she had imagined it to be inside – and more. Cosy, intimate, a perfect home for a newly married couple. She could have wept, thinking of what might have been. At least if she and Richard had married they would have had a similar little home surrounded by the beautiful countryside of the blue Virginian mountains. Life was too cruel. She shouldn't have come.

'And this is the conservatory we had built on for a dining room.'

'Good idea,' murmured Jane, being taken over the house to admire the three bedrooms, the small drawing room and new kitchen.

'Lovely, lovely,' was all she could murmur, conscious only of the close presence of Simon behind her.

As they came downstairs there was the roar of a powerful engine coming to a halt in the drive outside.

'What on earth is that?' Simon frowned.

Going to the front door he saw outside a brilliantly shiny new Harley-Davidson motor-cycle, its rider in leathers, taking off his helmet and goggles and coming towards them grinning from ear to ear.

'Gil!' he said. 'What on earth…?'

Gilroy Maclean looked proudly back at the machine glinting in the sunlight.

'Great, isn't she? I got her yesterday. Just had to bring her over to see you. Hope this isn't an inconvenient time, I could hardly take her to the office.' He stopped as he saw Susannah and another pretty girl he instinctively recognised standing in the doorway.

'Sorry old chap,' he said. 'I didn't realise you had guests.'

'We are showing Jane round – you remember Jane?' And a nerve began to twitch visibly in Simon's cheek.

'Of course.' Gil moved forward and took Jane's hand in his. He kissed Susannah and

275

turned back to Simon.

'Sorry to butt in, I won't stay. Just brought my newest acquisition over to show you.'

Susannah's eyes were shining. 'Oh, Gil, it's wonderful!'

'You like it? I didn't know you were a Harley-Davidson fan?'

'It's so beautiful – and new, Gil! Oh, how I would love a ride on it!'

'Would you?' He looked astonished.

'Look, come in, I'll make some tea.'

While she sorted out the tea things, Gil peeled off his gauntlets.

'I say, I'm awfully sorry to crash in. I should have thought you might have guests.'

His eyes were stern as he looked at Simon, and he recalled his confession to his friend just before the wedding.

'We've all been over to lunch at the Manor,' he said. 'Susannah's parents, and her aunt and uncle from America – Jane's parents,' he stressed.

Gil turned to her. 'Lovely, isn't it, the Dower House? Just perfect for a newly married couple,' he stressed, and Simon flushed.

'There!' Susannah placed a tray on the table, and poured from a silver teapot.

'I'm showing off the silver,' she explained.

'It was a wedding present from Simon's parents – only to be used on special occasions.'

'Very swish,' Gil said.

'Well, I never imagined I would serve tea to a leather-jacketed motor-cyclist in my own kitchen,' Susannah laughed.

I wonder if he was one of her boyfriends, too, Jane thought bitterly.

'I'll drink this and leave you,' Gil said.

'You're always welcome,' Susannah insisted.

'What's so special about a Harley-Davidson?' Jane asked, aware only of Simon's close proximity.

'It's only the greatest motor-cycle in the world.'

'Oh.'

'Our last contract helped to pay for this,' Gil explained.

'He spent his money on that instead of a wife.' Susannah smiled. 'I never knew you were so keen on motor-bikes, Gil.'

'Only Harleys – that was always one of my dreams.' He stood up. 'Well, having shown you, I must go.'

'Gil, could I possibly have a ride?' Susannah pleaded. 'Just a little way.'

He looked at Simon. 'Well, what about

your guest?'

'Oh, you wouldn't mind, would you, Jane?' begged Susannah.

'I think it's a bit rude to leave Jane,' Simon protested. 'Gil will come over some other time.'

Talking to me as if I were a child to be placated, Susannah thought.

'It's just for a minute or two,' she said, and thought, Anything to get away from dreary old Jane with her moody dark eyes.

'You'll need a helmet and something warm. It's quite cold at speed,' Gil warned her.

'Don't take her far,' Simon said. But Susannah had already run to get a riding hat and a leather jacket.

Simon and Jane watched until they were safely aboard the motor-cycle, then he came in and closed the door and took her firmly by the arms, almost shaking her.

'Why did you come?' he asked. 'How could you? You know how I feel about you...' And he took her in his arms and held her tight, bending down to kiss her. She turned her head. It was swimming.

'No, Simon, no! They might see ... oh, Simon, you don't know how I've longed for you. I've been so unhappy!'

'Me too,' he said. 'Jane, what are we going to do? I don't belong to Susannah, you know I don't.'

Her touch was like fire, her slim body yielding to his, her arms still around his neck when she broke away. 'We mustn't – oh, Simon!' Oh, it would be so easy. Then the distant sound of the engine came closer.

They broke apart and Jane went into the kitchen to stack the cups and saucers while Simon went out of the front door and called the two dogs to cover his confusion.

There they were coming slowly down the drive, Susannah's face flushed with excitement, cheeks rosy, lips parted. He hadn't seen her look like that for a long time. He helped her down from the bike.

'We only went to the bottom of the lane and back.' And Susannah and Simon walked back to the house.

'Oh, it was wonderful!' she said. 'Almost as good as hunting!'

She removed the hard hat and looked closely at Simon whose eyes were like steel.

'You didn't really mind, did you, darling?' she asked, her big blue eyes filled with devilment.

'Of course not,' he said stiffly.

Why do I feel I want to hurt him?

Susannah wondered, going into the house. I feel I want to shake him, shake some life into him, hurt him – so that it could be like it used to be.

She walked back into the house.

'Thanks, Jane, you shouldn't have.'

'My pleasure,' her cousin said politely.

There's something odd going on here, Susannah thought. I can almost feel the tension between those two. By golly, she's a devious little minx. But if she's after my husband, she's got another think coming.

She sighed deeply, then gave Jane a brilliant smile.

'Time we called the others, I think. Simon's just feeding the dogs.'

'Did you enjoy your ride?'

Susannah closed her eyes.

'Brilliant,' she said. 'Absolutely brilliant. You should try it some time. Gil's quite a catch, after all.'

Presently they were joined by Anne and Eric and Jane's parents, and Susannah made more tea while they all looked over the house.

'Well, darling,' her Aunt Felicity said. 'I must say it's all rather delightful – you are a very lucky girl.'

'I think she knows that,' Anne said proudly.

After tea, while Jane and Simon and Susannah walked the dogs, both sets of parents got ready to leave.

'I'm very glad we've been able to come over and visit,' Felicity said to her sister. 'Of course, we'll be off to Scotland on Tuesday and I still don't know whether Jane has decided to come with us. I have all the reservations, just in case. Still, we'll see.'

When the young people returned all of them were ready to go. They walked back to where the car was parked outside Fulford Manor and said their goodbyes.

'Have a wonderful time in Scotland. Are you going with them, Jane?' Susannah asked.

'Yes, of course,' she said as if it was a pre-ordained thing, and Felicity raised her eyebrows at Anne but looked relieved.

Anne waved from the car. 'Now, don't forget, you're coming to lunch next Sunday, Susannah and Simon. We'll give them all a proper send off. They'll be going back to the States on Monday.'

They waved from the car and Susannah and Simon walked back to the house.

Later that night in bed Susannah mulled over the visit. Her cousin Jane was a little disconcerting – always so quiet. But her fears had been unwarranted, she realised, the whole visit had gone very smoothly. How could Simon have seen anything in Jane anyway? The idea was ridiculous. Still, she wished she wasn't quite so bored with her marriage. Her husband lay lost in sleep beside her. It wasn't at all how she had imagined married life to be. They didn't seem to have fun any more.

Still, and her eyes shone in the dark, that had been a helluva run on Gil's motor-bike.

Chapter Fifteen

Early in July, Barbara woke to a brilliantly sunny morning, and flinging back the bedroom curtains looked out on a Birch Common where the trees were in full leaf and the roses in the tiny front garden in full bloom. Never again in the summer months to follow would there be quite so many roses – they were at their peak.

With a sense of excitement she made her way downstairs and prepared a hasty breakfast for she was expecting a visitor later.

Bryan was coming to lunch. It would not be the first visit, and each time he came here she felt their friendship grow stronger. In fact, she thought she was halfway in love with him, strange as it might seem at her age. It was certainly the closest she had felt to anyone since William died.

They would have a drink in the garden then go out to lunch at Bryan's suggestion – there was no point, he said, in Barbara spending time cooking when a restaurant was so close at hand.

This time he had driven over from Staines in his little Citroën, the car he kept for his free time. The motor-bike he kept for his work, it was reliable, fast and easy to park.

When he pulled up outside and parked the car, Barbara saw his tall figure walking up the path and felt a warm sense of familiarity. Then for no good reason she wondered what William would have thought of him. She decided he'd have considered Bryan a man's man ... And how lovely to be brought flowers.

When she opened the door, he kissed her and gave her the bouquet he had brought – white roses. Looking up at him, she met his eyes and wondered if he had remembered their walk in Kathmandu? The small boy and the white rose bush.

'Thank you. Come on in, we're out in the garden on this lovely day.'

He followed her through to the small garden where she had arranged chairs and table, with bits to nibble.

'I wasn't sure if you'd like gin and tonic or wine. Anyway, the white's in the fridge.'

'Oh, this is nice,' he said, sinking into a chair. 'I'll let you wait on me – and I'd like white wine. Shall I open it for you?'

'Yes, please, I'll bring it through.' She

thought how good it was to have a man around the house. He looked so right sitting there when she came back with the drinks tray.

'Are you off to Delhi tomorrow?' she asked when they were settled.

'No, not tomorrow. I've a week off and wondered if we might go out one day. What do you think?'

'I'd love to, but I'm working most days – well, I have Monday, Wednesday and Friday off but one of those I work half the day at the charity shop.'

'Which day would you prefer to meet me?'

'Wednesday? They're always pleased when I do Friday at the shop.'

'Make it Wednesday then. Shall we meet for lunch, say at twelve-thirty? After you've shopped or whatever.'

'I'd like to call in and see Rosemary, have coffee with her and meet you later. I'll give her a ring and see if she'll be there.'

Later they went to The Bear, eating in the pleasant dining room with its linenfold panelling and lovely outlook over the common.

'This place is very old,' Bryan said appreciatively.

'It used to be the haunt of highwaymen, so

I'm told. On the main road between here and Oxford – you can imagine.'

'I'm afraid my little house is nothing at all like yours,' he said looking across the common to where Barbara's was placed so invitingly. 'Pretty basic. Terraced – two up, two down – not too far from the airport.'

'That's all that matters then.' Barbara smiled.

'When we were first married, Lorna and I, we bought a nice little house at Hanwell. All mod cons, you know. We were there until she died then, somehow, I knew it wasn't right. It felt odd without her there, so I sold up and bought this little place in Staines.'

'And have you been there ten years?'

'Almost. Jenny and I – my daughter – until she moved out four years ago. She and Ian lived together first, trying it out as they say today, and married last year.'

He sat stirring his coffee. Barbara was dying to ask had he ever felt tempted to marry again, but knew she mustn't. It was an invasion of his privacy.

'It's awful, isn't it, when you're left after a happy marriage?' she said.

'Yes. I sometimes think it must be worse for a man but I'm not sure there's much in it, whichever way you look at it.'

'You know,' she began tentatively, 'that day when we first met I'd had a miserable time. I think I was at my lowest ebb. I'd wandered around Kensington feeling absolutely awful. I'd stayed overnight with Rosemary but it hadn't helped. Really I couldn't understand why, as time passed, I wasn't getting used to being without William. Then suddenly life opened up for me. I met you, and you mentioned India, and I remember thinking, why not? And I came home feeling all excited at the thought of doing something positive. That day I met Viv, my neighbour, for the first time. She's a dear, a good friend, and there's little Ben too, and a whole heap of other people. It made me realise that I'd led a sheltered life up to then.'

'Well, I have to admit, I hardly had time to grieve which was a good thing, though I was saddened to think of Lorna dying so young and not living to see her grandchildren – all of that. And I had a daughter to bring up which wasn't easy but my mother helped out there. Of course I was immersed in my work. There's nothing like travel and with its being my job I had to get on with it.'

'Is your mother still alive?'

'Yes, and still going strong. She's eighty and lives on her own quite happily.'

'And you meet a lot of people on your travels? Hardly any time for you to sit and mope.'

'Yes, I've made some good friends. One couple lived quite near here, in Beaconsfield. They came on the India trip. Sadly he died soon after. I went to see her, we'd become very friendly on the trip.'

Barbara felt deflated. Was this something he did often? Being a single man, did he make friends and visit them all, much as he was doing now? She had thought it was such a personal thing. Her imagination running away with her, perhaps.

'How is your daughter?' she asked brightly.

She saw his face light up and felt a twinge of jealousy. Bryan obviously adored Jenny. She saw those brown eyes twinkle. He had a rather craggy face, a strong mouth and a somewhat beaky nose. She liked a man to have a good nose. His teeth when he smiled were good too. He still had his hair, and his skin was, she imagined, permanently sunburned.

He smiled broadly. 'She's fine. Pregnant – did I tell you? I rather suspected she was.' He slipped his hand into his inside pocket and brought out a snapshot, handing it to Barbara.

She saw a pretty girl, brunette, very like her father to look at.

'She's like her mother,' Bryan said.

'I can see you there too,' Barbara said, handing it back.

He looked very pleased.

And I have no one, Barbara thought with a wave of self-pity. No one of my own.

'Well, I suppose we had better be getting back,' she suggested. 'Just time for a walk across the common, and home in time for tea.'

She collected her handbag and stood up, smiling across at him, and again he saw her grey-blue eyes and dark hair, not in any particular style. She obviously wasn't geared up to fashion in her light summer dress and open sandals. A slightly old-fashioned woman, he would have said, and all the better for it.

On Wednesday morning at ten-thirty Barbara arrived at Rosemary's house.

Her friend kissed her warmly. 'Lovely to see you. I've got the coffee on. We're all alone so we can have a chat.'

How long ago, Barbara thought, it seemed since she had left this house on that fateful morning, the one she'd thought she would break down, the morning that had changed her life.

Once seated round the kitchen table Barbara heard all Rosemary's news – how the children were doing at school, where they would go for their holidays. They were on their second cup of coffee before Rosemary addressed her directly.

'Now, I want to hear all *your* news. It sounded on the phone as if you are having quite a hectic time.'

'For me,' Barbara said. 'Yes.' And told her friend about her job at the bookshop, her charity commitments, leaving Bryan until the end.

'I saw Bryan on Sunday.'

'The courier?'

'Yes, he came over to lunch. We went to The Bear.'

'And?'

'Well, nothing really. He's good company. I like him, Rosemary.'

'I gathered that,' she said drily. 'And you are wondering whether – or if – you might get together?'

'Well, it seemed like it. Yet I got the impression that as a single man of ten years' standing he probably makes lots of friends whom he also visits – not just me.'

'Well, why shouldn't he? What's wrong with that?'

'I was thinking ... suppose he asked me to marry him, what would I say?'

'And what *would* you say?'

'I would have jumped at it at one time. But now–'

'Well, now,' Rosemary said practically, 'had you been younger – and I mean no offence – you would probably have jumped into bed together already.'

'Rosemary!'

'Well, you would. But I do sometimes wonder ... I mean, about hitching up again, marriage or otherwise. Barbara, you want company more than anything.'

'I like a man around the house,' Barbara said stolidly. 'It's comforting. At least it is to me.'

'Nothing wrong in that,' Rosemary said. 'But you see, Barbara, he's not going to be around the house much, is he? Off on his travels – two-week stints, aren't they? Home for a week and off again. Has it occurred to you that he might enjoy his life too much to want to tie himself down? It's different for you. What you want quite simply is a man around the house. A nine to fiver, that sort of man.'

'You make it sound so boring.'

'No, not if you're that kind of person. Some women, believe it or not, just do not want to be tied down to a man. They like their own company and are not about to take on the worry of a man – his laundry, cooking for him, and so on.'

'Well, I'm not like that. I get lonely... Although I'm not expecting to fall in love again, if that's what you mean.'

'Well, it helps to like the guy,' Rosemary said.

'I couldn't marry anyone just for the company. I'd have to like him, preferably love him. I mean, Rosemary, you're happy with Don, aren't you? And you've two children.'

'We're are as happy as sandboys,' her friend said. 'Seriously. But I wouldn't want you making a mistake, Barbara, just because you're temporarily lonely. All I'm saying is, think hard. Bye-bye, Bryan, on a Monday. Two weeks later home for a week then wave goodbye again.'

'Oh, you are horrible,' Barbara laughed, 'but I do see what you mean.'

'Wait a while. I think you have to feel more strongly than this, really I do,' Rosemary said. 'When does he retire?'

'Good Lord, I don't know! At sixty-five or maybe sixty. As long as he can keep going, I expect.'

'Well, think on, my girl.'

'I'm seeing him for lunch later.'

'Good. You need all the dates you can get. Just put him on your list. And what about this new bookseller you work for?'

'Tim? Oh, no!' Barbara cried.

'He's more your age, isn't he, early forties?'

'I don't see what that has to do with it,' she said. 'Besides,' she picked up her gloves, 'he has a boyfriend.'

'OK,' Rosemary reluctantly agreed, 'that does make a difference!'

As she neared the restaurant where they were to meet, Barbara could see through to the foyer where Bryan sat waiting for her. He looked so comfortably familiar, so William like, sitting there. His eyes were far away, though. What was he thinking?

He stood up when she came in.

'Ah, Barbara, glad you could make it.'

His eyes searched her face, then he beckoned to the waiter to take him to their table.

'How did you get on?'

'Oh, it was lovely seeing Rosemary again. She's my oldest friend and you don't need to waste time on trivialities with that sort of friendship, do you?'

He looked so solid and appealing, so comfortable in his tweed jacket, and his brown eyes were kind and warm.

'I've been walking most of the morning – I left home at nine,' he said.

'Walking where?'

'In the park. Two parks, in fact. It's a lovely time of the year. I wondered whether you would like to go to Hampton Court this afternoon?'

Her eyes shone. 'I'd love to.'

'Not in any hurry to get back?'

'No, my time is my own.'

During lunch Barbara was thinking hard. She was happier in this man's company than she was in anyone else's. She liked to be with a man, although she enjoyed women's company, but if she and Bryan married or lived together, for she was quite agreeable to their setting up house together on a trial basis, she would once more be living a lonely life with him away so much. For two weeks at a time, perhaps. Where would the fun be in that? And yet she knew if he walked out of her life, she would miss him more than somewhat.

Her thoughts were interrupted by the waiter who was asking what she would like for dessert.

She looked up, startled to find Bryan's eyes on her and was surprised by his understanding expression, almost as if he could read her thoughts.

They had been round the palace and were in the beautifully restored gardens, approaching the maze.

Bryan raised his eyebrows. 'Would you like to go round the maze?'

She shook her head in horror.

'No, thank you. I only did it once, and I was terrified.' Her eyes even now held a hint of the fear she had felt.

He took her hand in his and walked her over to a seat where they sat quite still, Bryan still holding her hand.

'Barbara, I know it's early days, but what would you think about us getting together – living together maybe, or what about marriage?'

'Bryan!' She was quite shocked by the speed of his proposal, hadn't expected it so soon.

'I'm quite sure of my feelings.' He smiled

fondly. 'I was wondering about yours. I've grown to like you very much, Barbara. In fact, I think I'm in love with you – probably have been since that day we first met.'

She looked into his brown eyes, her own swimming. 'I love you, too,' she said, then he bent forward and kissed her, the most wonderful kiss she could ever remember. When she broke away, oblivious to the people ambling by, seeing this middle-aged couple kissing on a park bench, she took his other hand.

'But living together – marriage,' she said. 'You're away so much and I get so lonely.'

'Darling,' he said, 'it would be only for two years. I'm forty-eight now and retire when I'm fifty, so if you could bear it until then...'

'Oh, Bryan! I didn't know you were that young ... I mean, you don't look your age ... I mean...'

'I'm travel-stained and weatherbeaten.' He laughed. 'So what do you think?'

'I'm forty-three,' Barbara said. 'Am I too old for you? I understood older men like younger women.'

'Some may,' he said. 'But, well, what do you say?'

'Oh, Bryan.'

'Another thing – you could come with me

on trips sometimes. And I have two weeks on, one week off, and a whole month's holiday. We could get reduced fares, travel anywhere you liked then.'

'Oh, you are the catch of the year!' she said, leaning forward and kissing him. He put his arms round her and held her tight until she gasped for breath.

Presently he sat back and talked seriously.

'First of all, why don't we have a weekend together – this coming weekend? Find a nice little hotel on the river, see how we get on, then we'll talk seriously about our future. What do you say?'

'What a lovely idea. Where shall we go?'

'Not too far. Can I take it we're officially engaged?'

'Oh, Bryan.' She put her arm through his.

'Let's go to Henley for the weekend,' he said.

It was Sunday, the day before the American visitors left for home, and they were due to arrive at Kirby Lodge for lunch.

While Susannah helped her mother in the house, Simon went to join her father in the garden. He seemed strangely on edge, had done so for the past few days.

Susannah wished the American relatives

weren't coming to lunch today. Far better if they had gone back straight from Scotland. Now she supposed they would have to hear all about that. She felt irritable, possibly at the thought of seeing Jane again. For some reason her cousin irked her. Aunt Felicity was fun, and Uncle Edwin a dear – but Jane, she was something else. The day was overcast, and rain was forecast, so it was not a propitious day for visitors.

They arrived around midday, and looked extremely well and fit after their holiday. Jane looked more rested, not so tense, her black polo neck sweater showing to advantage against her creamy swan-like neck, white tightly fitting trousers showing every inch of her slim figure. Her mane of dark curls was tied back, and those huge brown eyes were warm and soft as she greeted them.

When Eric and Simon joined them from the garden and greetings were exchanged, Susannah noted her husband greet her aunt first – and then her cousin Jane. She did not miss the swift glance they exchanged and once again experienced that momentary pang of shock and suspicion she had felt before. Next Simon shook hands with Edwin but the seed had been sown. Did they feel something for each other, these two? Was it hidden passion Simon felt for her unusual cousin? Why were her nerves set on edge every time she saw Jane? That she was an odd girl there was no doubt, but there was something else too. The atmosphere was almost charged when she and Simon were in a room together. That her suspicions should have any seed of truth in them was enough to send Susannah almost sky high with worry. She could hardly bear to be in the same room as them both.

'Well, now,' Anne said, 'let's go and sit in the drawing room, it's far too wet outside, and you can tell us all about it. Simon, help Eric with the drinks, would you?'

Susannah deliberately sat next to Jane so as to observe her closely. She seemed more forthcoming than usual, and spoke quite animatedly about the places they had visited in Scotland.

'Oh, I loved it,' she said enthusiastically, showing the first signs of animation since she had arrived. She talked of Edinburgh and how much it had changed. Her low voice with its sweet cadences made compulsive listening. Aunt Felicity sat back proudly as though to say, You see, Anne, *this* is what she's really like when she gets going, *this* is her normal self.

Susannah glanced at Simon, and saw that he was giving Jane his undivided attention. His grey eyes were fixed unblinkingly on her dark ones. Susannah could clearly read their expression. He was captivated, ensnared. It was like watching a rabbit in a trap.

The rest of the day passed like a dream. Luncheon, followed by a siesta for the visitors, Simon and her father reading the Sunday papers while her mother too rested. If only Susannah had the horses here she could have ridden.

She went upstairs to her old bedroom feeling utterly dispirited. Lying there, she mulled over how she had felt in the year since they were married – how dissatisfied Simon seemed to be, how dissatisfied she was herself. Had he fallen in love with Jane? Was he miserable because of that? Didn't he love her, Susannah, any more? She opened her book but couldn't read.

Well, she thought at length obstinately, I am his wife, whatever he feels. He's mine – and perhaps after all I'm only imagining it. But there is something wrong ... suppose, just suppose, he has fallen for her. Like one of those sudden fall-in-love things you read about and which she was sure did not happen very often. But might have. Well, much good may it do you, Jane, my girl! Thank God she was going back to the States tomorrow. And that would be that.

It was one of the strangest Sundays Susannah had ever spent. Their visitors began packing in the evening ready for the early start to Heathrow in the morning. She and Simon were about to start making tracks for home.

When Susannah came out of her room some time later, she passed the room that Jane had and heard muffled sounds. She stood rooted to the spot then tapped gently and tried the door – but it was locked. She was sure she could hear a man's voice inside. Simon with Jane? Who else could it be? She felt sick inside and hurried away as though she herself had done something wrong.

Anne, coming through the hall, met her coming down the stairs.

'Why, you're trembling, darling. Are you cold? You look as if you've seen a ghost. Are you all right?'

'Just a bit queasy, that heavy lunch, I think. Where is everyone?'

'We're waiting for them to come down – are you sure you and Simon won't stay for a while?'

'No, thank you, Mummy. We must get back. Simon has to be off early in the morning.'

In the drawing room they waited for everyone to appear. Goodbyes were said, and hugs given.

'Thanks for coming over,' Felicity said, 'it's been lovely seeing you all.' And everyone shook hands, Jane and Simon coolly, not kissing.

Then Simon and Susannah were in the car, and he had barely left the drive before he stopped the car on the green.

'Susannah,' he said, looking straight at her. His jaw was working. 'I've something to tell you.'

She turned her bright eyes to him as inspiration came from nowhere.

'And I have something to tell you!' she said, eyes brimming.

He stared at her.

'You have?'

'Darling – I'm pregnant!' she said. 'Isn't it wonderful?'

Chapter Sixteen

Barbara and Bryan arrived at the hotel in Henley at lunchtime, having driven down from Birch Common late morning. The hotel was small and by the river. Not many rooms, cosy with its oak beams and warm with welcome.

They went down to lunch almost immediately and sat in the bar overlooking the river, watching the ducks and swans and moorhens. Barbara couldn't have been happier. She had prepared for this brief holiday almost as if she were going on honeymoon, going through her wardrobe to find something suitable to wear. The dress and jacket she had worn on the Indian trip were suitable but she'd decided to splash out on a new nightie and found one eventually, palest blue silk and lace with a matching wrap.

It was a long time since she had been so happy. After lunch they walked through the Henley streets, looking at the antique shops in one of which Bryan insisted on buying her a Victorian ring, a golden citrine surrounded by tiny diamonds.

'I love it,' Barbara said, and wore it on her right hand although she had already removed her wedding ring from her left hand together with her former engagement ring.

Bryan had put it on her right hand. 'It's up to you, Barbara,' he said. 'Your choice.'

'When we go to India again,' she said, 'I'd like a bracelet just like one of those Toni Thing used to wear, do you remember?'

'I remember the bracelets – but I'd rather not remember Toni Thing.'

After dinner they went to their room, and once in the bathroom Barbara found herself feeling very nervous. It had been such a long time, and she had never known the love of any man other than William. Bryan was very different.

She was in bed when he came in from the bathroom and she knew at once from his expression that it was going to be all right. He lowered himself beside her and she switched off the overhead light.

'Lovely Barbara,' he whispered, and she put both arms round his neck and drew him down to her.

'I don't believe you!' Viv said when Barbara told her the news. 'Marry him?' She threw an astonished glance at Barbara's happy face. 'Barbara, are you sure this is what you want?'

'Quite sure,' she said tranquilly. 'Oh, Viv, don't look so worried!'

'Well, it seems so sudden. After all, you've hardly known him that long.'

'Long enough,' Barbara said. 'And we're neither of us getting any younger. We went away for the weekend and it was wonderful.'

Viv went over and hugged her. 'Then I'm glad, really I am. It's just that I couldn't bear to see you hurt. You've already had one tragedy.'

She went over and made the coffee, coming back to the table with it.

'Now tell me all about it. What exactly did he say? Where were you? I'm a bit of a romantic at heart though you may not believe it.'

'At Hampton Court,' Barbara said dreamily. 'He'd just asked me if I wanted to go into the maze, and when I shivered at the thought, he took my hand in his and the next minute we were sitting on a seat and he was asking me to marry him.'

'Fast mover,' Viv said admiringly.

Barbara smiled.

'And you had no doubts? You know, about his going away and all that.'

'We haven't worked anything out yet, we behaved like a couple of teenagers actually, but it will work out, Viv. I shall make it work.'

She looked so determined, Viv was sure that she would.

'We're not getting married right away, we're going to give it a try, first, but I have no doubts at all. Bryan retires in two years so that'll work out, and he says sometimes I can travel with him.'

'But where will you live?'

'For the time being, we'll share. I'll go up to Staines sometimes and at other times Bryan will come here. I'm just so lucky to have met someone like him, Viv.'

'Ye-es,' she said slowly. 'I think you are.'

'But tell me about you and George? I've been thinking about you so much. He's gone back now, hasn't he?'

She looked so anxious that Viv laughed.

'Only temporarily.' She smiled smugly. 'He'll be back for good at the end of the week.'

'Oh, that's wonderful! How did it happen? I can see by your expression you feel you've won him over.'

'Well, no, not exactly, but almost as soon as he got home, after dinner on that first night, he told me the options were open for him to do another stint in Florida, or go to Kingston Ontario for two years.'

'He must be incredibly good at his work,' Barbara observed.

'I think he is – but the wonderful thing is, Barbara, he opted for coming home! I was so pleased. I really missed him, but wasn't going to admit it.'

'What about Peter?' Barbara asked.

'Well, I told him over the phone that George and I were getting back together – and he didn't seem surprised. Said he wished he and his ex could do the same. I liked him, Barbara. Nice man. Ben said to George, "Peter couldn't come today," and George said, "Who's Peter?" Ben just said, "He's a friend of ours," and no more was said. As for my mother, she's walking around like a dog with two tails.'

'Well, I'm delighted,' Barbara said. She had so longed for them to get back together again.

'So – what will George do?'

'Well, it definitely won't be Florida or Kingston,' and she winked.

'Oh, you are naughty!' said Barbara.

'Well, he can always do a stint over there when Ben is older, he knows that, and I might even go with him then – but no promises. Shall we indulge in a piece of my mother's cake?'

The visit to Bryan's daughter was a great success. It happened two weeks later on one of his home stints and Barbara was more than a little nervous.

She had some idea what Jenny was like from the snapshot, but now, driving down the neat little suburban avenue, Barbara found she was feeling quite anxious. Would Jenny like her? Would she approve of her father's bride-to-be?

They stopped outside a neat little semi-detached house in a leafy avenue with a front garden full of flowers. After giving her hand a squeeze, Bryan rang the bell.

Jenny answered the door, looking just like her picture but prettier, obviously pregnant and delighted to be so.

'Dad.' She kissed him, and then smiled. 'So this is Barbara.'

Barbara gave her the bouquet of flowers she had brought, and thought, It's going to be all right.

'Thank you.' Jenny led the way into the sitting room, a very modern room with polished wooden floors and minimalist furniture. She smiled as they sat down. 'Well, I knew it had to happen one day. Excuse me while I see to the coffee and put these flowers in water.'

She disappeared and Barbara gave a relaxed smile. 'There, I told you it was going to be all right,' Bryan said.

His daughter reappeared with the coffee.

'I've been hoping for Dad to meet someone for a long time,' she said, pouring it out. 'How long have you been a widow?'

'Nearly three years.'

'Dad's been alone for ten,' Jenny said, sipping her coffee. 'And, of course, his job has been a lifeline – I don't know what he'd have done without that.'

Barbara glanced over towards the low table where there was a picture of a couple smiling happily. The woman was an older version of Jenny, pretty and petite. I've a lot to live up to, Barbara thought, I hope he will be happy.

'Do you have a job, Barbara? You're going to be lonely when Dad's away.'

'She'll come with me sometimes,' he said, and Barbara gave him a swift look. He had meant it then.

'And where will you live?' Jenny asked, then laughed. 'I sound like a father interviewing the prospective bridegroom – I don't mean to be nosy, but I'm just so pleased and want Dad to be happy. He deserves it. He's been a great father to me.'

She was so like him that Barbara felt an instant rapport with her. Another friend, she thought. After all, Bryan's child could have disliked me on sight. She gave a fleeting thought as to whether this was the first time since her mother's death Jenny had had this task to do, then rejected it. I must live for the future, she told herself, and realised she would be acquiring a stepdaughter and later a grandchild. The prospect gave her enormous pleasure.

Jenny gave them a light lunch, and afterwards showed them over the house and small garden.

'Well, when's it going to be?' she asked.

'What? Oh, the wedding.' Barbara flushed. She looks really pretty, Jenny thought, with some colour in her cheeks.

Bryan looked at Barbara, and Jenny could see that there was no doubt as to his feelings for her and felt a surge of thankfulness. She had thought sometimes this moment would never come, that he would grow into an elderly widower living on his own. Now she could dismiss that fear.

'As long as you don't clash with the baby,' she said, looking down at her swollen tum. 'I want to dress up for this wedding.'

'When is it due?' Barbara asked.

'Christmas!' Jenny laughed. 'It can't get more inconvenient than that, can it?'

'The wedding all depends on Bryan's commitments,' Barbara said.

They drove away from Jenny's house, smiling and waving. Round the corner, Bryan pulled in to a convenient space.

'Well,' he said. 'That went all right, didn't it?' And kissed Barbara.

She took his hand. 'Bryan, she's a super girl. You must be so proud of her.'

'I am,' he said. 'As proud as I shall be of my new wife.' Oh, yes, Viv, Barbara told herself. I am doing the right thing. I know I am.

It wasn't going to be easy, Susannah told herself. She had been totally oblivious of the repercussions when she'd blurted out to Simon that she was pregnant. She couldn't really get away with it – how could she hope to? She was playing for time, no more, no less.

And Simon had looked so pleased! Had put his arms around her and held her close, all thought of what he had been about to say gone from his head.

Oh, but she was wicked! It had been an act of pure desperation. Sure that he was about to tell her of his love for Jane, she had said almost the first thing that came into her head to prevent him, knowing it would stun him.

Well, it had done that all right. First the shock, then the pleasure, and inside her all the time the dreadful worry: What do I do now? For there was no way she could get away with it.

When he stopped hugging her, she followed through with the first thing that came into her head.

'Darling, we will keep it our secret for now, won't we?' He looked disappointed.

'But the parents?'

'We can tell them later.'

'Are you sure? How do you know for certain…'

'I did a test,' she said, lying again, and he hugged her. I wish, I wish, she thought miserably.

'I can't believe it,' Simon said.

Her mind was in turmoil. She'd successfully prevented him from saying what he'd been about to tell her, but she was no longer in any doubt as to what that was. Simon loved Jane and had been about to confess it to her.

Oh, what an awful dilemma! At some point, unless she could become pregnant the next month, he would find out she'd been deceiving him, and what would he do then? Thoughts and fears ran round and round her head.

She looked so crestfallen that he took her in his arms again.

'Darling, you are pleased, aren't you? There's nothing wrong?'

'No, of course not.'

'Have you seen a doctor?'

'I've hardly had time,' she said, somewhat sharply. 'I only did the test today.'

He buried his face in her hair.

'You can't know how pleased I am,' he said softly.

Perhaps he wasn't going to tell me about Jane, she thought miserably. But he was, I know he was. Well, if this is all it takes, he couldn't have felt that strongly about her.

'I can't wait to tell everybody,' he said.

'Later, darling, let's keep it to ourselves for now. Please, Simon?'

'Just as you say,' he soothed her. He took a deep breath, and started up the car. 'Home, then,' he said, and all the way back Susannah wondered what he was thinking.

Once there, they talked of nothing else but the coming baby until she could have screamed. Later that night, in bed, after making love, she knew he lay awake beside her, as unable to sleep as she herself.

God, what a mess.

After the first shock of Susannah's news, Simon adjusted to the situation. Saying farewell to Jane had been the hardest thing he had ever done, and he had decided to make a clean breast of it to Susannah – there seemed no point in their continuing a marriage when one of them was in love with someone else. He had decided to burn his boats and leave his wife. From his point of view the marriage was a mockery, which was hard on Susannah because he knew she loved him. But better to break now than continue living a lie.

The baby changed everything. Not only for them, but for his parents and the Rawns-ley line. An heir. His mother would be delighted, as would his father, but Susannah wished it to be kept secret. 'Until three

314

months,' she'd said. 'Then we can be sure.

He couldn't see her line of reasoning but accepted that perhaps some women had odd whims when they were pregnant, so gave in. Susannah certainly didn't seem to behave like other mothers-to-be. She felt well, she said, had no problems, and apart from wanting to make love as often as they could, was her normal self. Slightly irrational, a little bored, but then that was how she'd been ever since they had married.

At the time that her period became due she went to stay with her parents at Birch Common for a couple of days. It arrived as usual, she wept and wondered what she was going to do now. She did the same thing a month later and wondered if she was going mad, acting like this.

She had decided she must have a miscarriage, as far as Simon was concerned, and was relieved as the third month approached when he announced he was going up to Scotland for two or three days to finalise the Scottish contract.

'Are you sure you'll be all right?' he asked her.

'Of course I will,' she said. 'Your mother is close at hand.' She was almost beginning to believe in this pregnancy herself, one lie following another.

She relaxed on the first day of his departure. Now that she had time to work out some sort of solution she realised that to feign a miscarriage was not going to be easy. A doctor must be called, Simon would insist. If she went home to Birch Common, he would go with her. All in all, the whole thing was a deceitful, terrible mess, and she wished with all her heart she had never started it in the first place.

Lying with a book on the sofa around five o'clock on the day of Simon's return, she heard the sound of an engine outside on the drive. It could hardly be Simon's car making that racket. Going to the window, she saw leather-clad Gil on his Harley-Davidson, and her heart leapt.

She reached the door as he knocked and, opening it, nearly fell into his arms.

'Oh, Gil! Gil! I'm so pleased to see you!'

'Hi, there!' he said. 'Missing him that much? Well, well.'

He pushed the door to behind him with his foot as she clung to him.

'What's up?' he asked.

She broke away, and looked up at him. 'Nothing wrong, is there? Nothing happened to Simon?'

'No, he's all right. I brought some mail – here.' And he put it down on the side table.

She took his arm. 'Oh, come in, come in, Gil. I'm in terrible trouble.'

Her face was as white as a sheet.

'Sit down,' he said. 'Now what is it? Nothing can be that bad, surely? Are you ill?'

'I've done something awful.'

'Slept with another man?' he prompted her.

'No – I'm going to have a baby. I mean, I'm *not* going to have a baby but–'

He felt so sorry for her. She seemed to be beside herself. He wanted to take her in his arms.

'Start again, I'm confused.'

She took a deep breath.

'Well, I told Simon I was pregnant – and I wasn't,' she confessed.

Gil looked serious.

'When was this?'

'Some time ago. I should be two and a half months by now.'

'And you're not?'

She shook her head miserably.

'Oh, Susannah, why did you do it?'

She burst into tears. 'I thought he was going to leave me for Jane.'

'Leave you for Jane?' Gil repeated. Surely

that wasn't still going on? His eyes were like steel. 'What made you think that?'

'Well, you know when they came to stay? It was pretty obvious then he was in love with her. The night we'd said goodbye to her, he stopped the car and said, "I've something to tell you." And I knew what he was going to say so...' She gulped and continued, 'I said I was pregnant. It was the only way I could think of to hold him. Things haven't been the same between us since we married, Gil.'

'So you told him you were pregnant.' His voice was grim.

Poor little thing! The lengths to which some women would go for a man. And he wished, not for the first time, that he was that man for Susannah. He was shocked that Simon still hankered after the other girl – she had left him cold personally but there was no accounting for taste. That Susannah should go through all this ... of her own making, true, but she didn't deserve this.

'Now sit up and dry your eyes. You look awful,' he said bracingly. She did as she was told and gave him a watery smile.

'Oh, I'm so glad I've told you.'

'Yes, but now you have something else to do. You must tell Simon.'

318

'Oh, I couldn't!'

''Fraid you have to. It's the only way. What did you intend to do?'

'I thought I might have a miscarriage – lose the baby somehow.'

'And compound the felony? Oh, no. Be honest with him. I'm sure he'll understand your reasons.' But at heart he had his doubts. There was a core of steel in Simon deep down.

He looked at his watch.

'Look, you need a stiff drink. When do you expect Simon to get back?'

'Around eight, I think.'

He went over and poured a glass of red wine for Susannah, a gin and tonic for himself.

'You are a little goose.'

'I know,' she admitted. 'Did you know or suspect about Jane?'

He shook his head. He felt he couldn't reveal to Susannah what Simon had told him on the eve of their wedding. It wouldn't be fair.

'I never really saw her that much. I'm sure you're wrong.'

'Oh, no,' she said fervently. 'I'm not.'

'Just think about what you're going to say. You can't possibly go ahead with the miscarriage idea. Come clean.'

'It's easy for you, you haven't got to do it. Can you imagine Simon's face when I tell him? Oh, Gil, I can't!' And she collapsed against his chest. He put down his glass and held her close.

You can always come to me, he wanted to say. I would love you dearly – I always have. He put her away from him, smoothing her hair away from her face.

'You can depend on me,' he said lightly. 'I'll help you out, Susannah. Drink up and think about what you're going to say. But be honest, it's the best way. If I know old Si, he'll understand.'

'He won't,' she said bitterly.

'Look, I have to go now but I'll give you a ring tomorrow. Everything will be all right then.' He kissed her lightly. 'Be brave.'

What a good friend Gil was. If she hadn't been able to talk to someone, she would have burst. Thinking of Simon and Jane, she wondered how deep their feelings ran, whether it had all started when they first met. Had her marriage to him been a sham all along? Had he wanted to be in Jane's arms all the time he had been married to her? Susannah shuddered. I should never have told that lie, she thought. I should never have had to use such an excuse to hold on to him. Surely I have more pride than that? She made up her mind. She would tell him as soon as he came home.

She poured herself another drink to give herself courage, then another ... then another...

When Simon came in at eight-thirty he found her asleep on the sofa. He saw the empty wine bottle and glass on the table, and touched her gently.

'Susannah?'

She opened her eyes slowly, unable to focus, then realisation dawned. 'Oh, Simon! Oh, no!' She buried her head in the cushions.

He shook her. 'Are you all right, Susannah?'

'I've had a lot to drink,' she whispered. 'Too much.'

'But should you?' he asked. 'Isn't it bad for the...'

'The baby? Yes, of course it is, but there isn't going to be a baby!' she almost shouted.

He looked stricken. 'Not going to be a baby? You mean, you've miscarried ... oh, darling!' He put his arms around her.

Here was her chance. But she pushed him

away and sat up straight.

'No. I made it up.'

He stared at her.

Her blue eyes wide, she stared back.

'You made it up,' he said slowly, as if there was no way he could believe it.

'Yes, I made it up.' Her fingers picked nervously at a cushion. 'I thought you were going to leave me for – for Jane—and I thought that would stop you.'

He stood up and walked over to the window, standing with his back to her.

'I can't believe you would do such a thing,' he said, turning round to face her. But it was true, he thought, everything falling into place. Like not wanting her in-laws or her parents to know.

He came over and stood looking down at her.

'How can you say you love me and do a thing like that?'

She shook her head. 'I do love you. I didn't want you to leave me. Is it true about Jane? Are you in love with her?'

His lip curled. 'You don't know the meaning of the word,' he said, and turning on his heel went out of the room.

Susannah collapsed into tears again, finally climbing into bed exhausted. She thought

Simon must be in the spare room. But by the morning, he had gone.

He slept at his parents' house, and knew what he had to do next. In the morning he would tell them. He had lived a lie too long. They would be devastated, but it couldn't be helped. It was Jane he loved, and she loved him. They belonged together. Although the news would hurt many people he was prepared to go through with it.

He glanced at his watch and saw the time. From his father's study he put a call through to Jane, finally catching up with her in Virginia.

'It's over,' he said. 'I'm on my way.'

Chapter Seventeen

At the charity shop Barbara was standing in for Doris who was on holiday. It was a Monday morning and she waited outside for Gladys with the key. Once inside it was all go. Doors were unlocked, windows thrown open, and a general assault made on the storeroom.

'Pink and blue window scheme!' Gladys called loudly. 'Find me pinks and blues and I'll do the window. That blue frock will do over there, and do we have a large pink hat? Blue will do if not. Get me that pink skirt off the rail, Ba. Oh, and that pink and blue striped jumper. Annie, look in that box in the kitchen for a handbag. It'll have to be navy, I expect. And that bunch of pink roses – lovely. Now, more pink and blue. Look sharp, ladies.'

She had them all running around until the window was finished, and Barbara had to admit it did look nice.

When the shop opened at nine-thirty, the usual first-comers trailed in. The woman

324

with the baby, the large woman who went straight to the underclothes section, the elderly lady who always went for the books, the young man who made for men's suits. It was the mixture as before.

It was around half-past ten when the door was opened by a man who looked vaguely familiar to Barbara. He came in carrying a large, long box which obviously held something rather special. He looked slightly uncomfortable and Barbara pointed towards the storeroom door which stood open.

Gladys was there immediately.

'Oh, thank you, sir,' she said. She was always very polite. 'This looks very promising.'

He left hurriedly, glad to get out.

When the shop had emptied a little Barbara made her way to the room where Gladys was just unpacking the box.

Inside was a wedding dress, a really beautiful wedding dress complete with headdress. No veil. As Gladys unwrapped the tissue paper its full glory was revealed. She held it against herself. 'Tall girl,' she said. 'Lovely figure.' And looked at the inside neck. 'Hélène,' she read. 'Never 'eard of 'er. Still, it's a good one. We'll put it back in its box, it's safer like that.' And all hands on deck, the precious dress was folded and put back into its box.

Later in the morning it came to Barbara that the person who had brought it was the chauffeur at Kirby Lodge. Could it have been the daughter's wedding dress... Susannah Whittaker that was?

It was sold a week later to a young girl who came in with her mother. The girl was obviously pregnant, and very young, and looked really miserable. But Mother was in charge and she wanted a proper wedding dress. Gladys looked doubtful, but then she always did and highly disapproved of young girls getting pregnant before they were married. Still, duty was duty. She fetched the wedding dress out on its hanger.

She held it grimly in front of herself and saw the mother's eyes gleam. Gladys knew she was going to have it long before she knew it herself.

'I don't know if she'll get into it,' she said, not mincing her words. Gladys never did. The girl looked worried.

'Can she try it on?' the mother asked.

'Of course.'

So inside the cubicle mother and daughter went, where the wedding dress took up most of the space. The mother pushed the daughter out once dressed and she stood before the long mirror, having given the wedding dress life despite her condition. It was too long, and too tight, but you knew the mother was not going to pass it over on that account.

'How much is it?' she asked.

'Forty quid,' Gladys said, not blinking an eyelid.

'I'll have it,' the woman said.

It was early September and Constance Pargetter-Wilson had been home a week from attending her son's wedding in Hong Kong – and what an experience that had been! She still couldn't believe it. The flight out to Hong Kong, the arrival at Mai Ling's luxurious home, a whole new Chinese family to meet and befriend.

The wedding had been wonderful. There had been tears in her eyes as she'd watched her tall handsome son make his vows beside the diminutive Mai, who looked adorable in her magnificent wedding gown. The look she gave Dennis as she finally flung her bridal veil back from over those dancing black eyes was devastating. Constance had wiped away a surreptitious tear. And afterwards at the reception at a grand and glorious hotel – well, there'd been food such as she had never tasted in her life. Even Geoffrey was impressed. Oh, it had been dreamlike, but still, she had all the photographs to prove it.

It was only today she'd finally come down to earth at a meeting in aid of the local children's home. She'd wound up the proceedings in her usual crisp way and glanced surreptitiously at her watch. Today was Friday, and this evening was the one night of the week she had all to herself. What with committee meetings all the week, for schools and various charities, she had insisted early on that one evening a week must be her very own. Geoffrey had agreed with her for he attended most of the evening meetings with her and knew what a toll it exacted on one's personal life.

Arriving home around five in the afternoon, she changed, brushing and hanging her suit on its hanger, putting the blouse and her tights aside for washing then slid into slippers and housecoat.

She had bathed by five-thirty and made herself a cup of tea to drink before getting dressed again. Now she sat at her dressing table looking into the mirror. In a small silver bowl stood a single dark red rose, almost in full bloom, its scent perfect. She held it to the side of her face, then picking up a small brocade box took off the lid to expose a red silk rose, a perfect replica of the real thing. She had bought it in Hong Kong. It was exquisitely made, but she replaced it in its box, put the lid back on and picked up the real rose again to sniff its scent. Yes, that was the one. She began to put together her make-up and a small attaché case of things she'd need and by six-thirty was on her way.

It was an hour's journey before Constance finally arrived at her destination, an ugly breeze-block building with green-painted entrance doors and a neon sign flashing and lighting up a banner which read TONIGHT AT NINE. Constance walked up the stone steps where an elderly man sat in a reception booth.

'Evening, Margot,' he said.

'Evening, Tom,' she replied, and made her way to the locker room which was packed with other women.

'Hi, Margot, how's it going?'

She hung up her coat and dress and sat in her slip at a dressing table encircled with light bulbs, taking down her long hair which fell almost to her waist. She brushed it hard with regular strokes, jet black hair with no trace of grey. It was glossy by the time she had finished and she pulled it back straight from her brow and wound it into a chignon, pinning it closely to her head with strong hairpins so that it would not come loose. Finally she tucked in the red, red rose. Then came the creams, smoothing her skin until she was satisfied, and the make-up, quite heavy, most of it going on her eyelids and below. Then the false eyelashes, each glued individually in place, and the shiny scarlet lipstick.

There was movement all around her, girls and women coming and going, the sound of music and announcements over the microphone. The room was almost empty when she changed into her own costume – first her lacy stockings which she smoothed over her legs, then a short black velvet gown, cut tight to show all her curves and the smooth skin of her arms, which were firm and silky, the dress's thin straps showing her magnificent shoulders. Her nails were scarlet talons, and her shoes sparkling with diamante on the highest heels you had ever seen.

She looked fantastic, and she knew it. With a little smile she left the dressing room and was met outside by her partner, Rafael. He was tall, handsome and Spanish-looking.

'You look smashing, Margot,' he whispered, and as the orchestra struck up the languorous strains of a tango and the lights dimmed they appeared on the floor with two other couples. She looked imperious, heels stamping, fingers snapping, but light as a feather – he held her, threw her away, caught her. Her head was flung back, scarlet mouth moving provocatively beneath his – never had the crowd seen anything more exciting and sexy than this beautiful woman who danced like a dream.

'MISS MARGOT ROMAYNE AND MR RAFAEL BATINI!'

To shouts of applause and stamping of feet they took their bows, winners for the fourth time of the Tango Final. Rafael kissed her briefly and, carrying a huge bouquet of flowers, she made her way back to the dressing room.

Opening the door of her locker, she placed a silver trophy carefully inside and began to disrobe, to cream her face, remove the make-up and the rose, while all the time her dark eyes smiled.

Once outside, she saw Rafael with his friend, Anton.

'Hello, there, Anton.'

'You was brilliant, Margot,' he said, and

she smiled.

'Thank you. All credit due to Rafael, as you know.' She watched as arm in arm they left the building to celebrate.

She made her way back to the car park and set off on the hour-long journey home. It was two in the morning, and Geoffrey was asleep in bed, when she finally came in. He stirred sleepily.

'How was your mother?'

'Oh, just fine,' Constance said, yawning. 'Everything's fine.'

The publishers hope that this book has given you enjoyable reading. Large Print Books are especially designed to be as easy to see and hold as possible. If you wish a complete list of our books please ask at your local library or write directly to:

Magna Large Print Books
Magna House, Long Preston,
Skipton, North Yorkshire.
BD23 4ND

This Large Print Book, for people
who cannot read normal print,
is published under the auspices of

THE ULVERSCROFT FOUNDATION

... we hope you have enjoyed this book.
Please think for a moment about those
who have worse eyesight than you ...
and are unable to even read or enjoy
Large Print without great difficulty.

You can help them by sending a
donation, large or small, to:

**The Ulverscroft Foundation,
1, The Green, Bradgate Road,
Anstey, Leicestershire, LE7 7FU,
England.**
or request a copy of our brochure for
more details.

The Foundation will use all donations
to assist those people who are visually
impaired and need special attention
with medical research, diagnosis
and treatment.

Thank you very much for your help.